When Mira
Forth and Multiplied

Shinie Antony has written three collections of short fiction –
Barefoot and Pregnant, Planet Polygamous and *Séance on a Sunday
Afternoon.* She has compiled the anthologies *Kerala, Kerala, Quite
Contrary* and *Why We Don't Talk.* This is her second novel.

Praise for previous work

Shinie Antony is a gifted writer...she has absolutely no interest in
feel-good presentations

– The Hindu

Antony's quality to not just put herself in the shoes of her characters
but to become one with them is creditable

– Deccan Herald

Often atrocious, often outrageous, often dark, but funny all the time

– The New Indian Express

Séance on a Sunday Afternoon by Shinie Antony is about 'things that go
bump in the mind'. The short stories are startling in their cheekiness
and black humour

– The Telegraph

Zany, inventive, sardonic, deliciously irreverent

– The Week

The febrile, edgy voice haunts the reader's imagination with a peculiar
force of conviction

– Biblio

Barefoot and Pregnant is an excellent counterweight to the excessively sentimental fiction about mothers that is more commonly found. It is an unusual set of stories about a side of motherhood that is rarely featured: sometimes moving, sometimes startling, sometimes unnerving, and sometimes tragic

– Outlook.com

The lightness of tone is kept skin-deep as Shinie Antony takes us into worlds that are about to stop ticking

– IANS

A heady mix of slapstick and sadism

– India Today

Shinie Antony is brave enough to move away from the usual style of writing to create her own

– The Financial Express

In her third collection, *Séance on a Sunday Afternoon*, Shinie's at it again. If there's a literary equivalent to the minimalist artist, it is she. She manages startling nuances with a juxtaposition, twist or unusual usage. Her characters reach the edge of expected behaviour only to go into a slew of surprises. With few words she swiftly forges resonant implications

– Shreekumar Varma, The Times of India

When Mira Went
Forth and Multiplied

Shinie Antony

Rupa & Co

Published 2011 by
Rupa Publications India Pvt. Ltd.
7/16, Ansari Road, Daryaganj,
New Delhi 110 002

Sales Centres:

Allahabad Bengaluru Chennai
Hyderabad Jaipur Kathmandu
Kolkata Mumbai

Printed in India by
Rekha Printers Pvt Ltd.
A-102/1, Okhla Industrial Area, Phase-II,
New Delhi-110 020

to Mariam, my grandmother

That howsoever people fast and pray,
The flesh is frail, and so the soul undone.

−*Don Juan*, Byron

1

On a midsummer midmorning a woman in her mid-thirties simply forgot her manners. 'I want to be the @%** sort,' she bellowed bang in the middle of the road, uncaring that two buses, one kindergarten mini-van and a Horn-OK-Please lorry had to quickly brake.

'Get this straight,' she addressed mankind in general, 'I'm talking solid, money-in-the-bank, bulletproof beauty to slam men cross-eyed into walls. *That* type of woman.'

The rapidly gathering audience switched off their mobiles and waited most attentively for her to do what madwomen traditionally did – take off her clothes. The sun quit the sky for a bit, bullied by its own clouds, and a breeze unpinned her hair. Frizz flew into her eyes, mouth, everywhere, helping her behold them as they materialised before her, the spirits of femmes fatales.

They came haunting on high heels, these bad-girl ghosts, mostly as she had pictured them, with billowing hair and not a stitch on them. Pale wraiths with slit wrists, tarts and trollops with their panty lines showing, sultry sirens blowing smoke, mistresses and keeps with arch smiles, sex kittens, harlots and size-zero starlets, chasing up cads and cocktails, with come-hither eyes and lips all parted in a moue.

'Make me,' she begged them, 'you.' Strung along all her adult life with promises of muscle tone and a swan-like neck, she was applying for change, body and soul. She'd pray for world peace when she was beauty queen, but right now, God knew, she needed some oomph.

Wait a minute. Was she praying to the right authorities, in the right place, at the right time? Statues of gods, saints and great men riding horses had a divine fortitude about them she instantly trusted; darting into a temple/church to return the granite gaze of a well-graven god was a given. The God of Groins got even with fungal thunderbolts. Surely there was a god who'd make her armpits rain deodorant...

A traffic policeman personally escorted her off the road with the exaggerated courtesy reserved for the mentally unsound. 'You cannot stop like that in the traffic, madam,' he mumbled, not quite meeting her eye. Small talk with the insane was not on police curriculum.

'I did not,' she clarified through gritted teeth. 'My scootie did.'

He looked back at her rigor mortised scootie like he expected it to rebut. Then he turned to her, 'And you cannot talk on mobile, madam, while driving.'

'I was talking,' she said with dignity, 'to myself'. She stood as law-abidingly as she knew how to by the pavement while he went back for her scootie, and upon his return, obliged him with a high-pitched laugh. He seemed to expect it and stereotypical mad was no big deal. She was born with stir-fry hair and his deference did crack her up.

He placed the strawberry-pink scootie by the roadside. Okay, not strawberry pink, more like someone had tried to eat a particularly inedible artificially ripened off-season fruit and puked all over her only means of transport. She uprighted it with a broad smile, remains of that glorious laugh still in her mouth, thinking Wednesday a perfect day to go bonkers.

Dreams had yanked Mira Jacob out of Kozhikode eight years ago even as her mother wailed, father fumed and well-wishers clicked their tongues. In the end Mr Jacob, who had run in slow motion towards Mrs Jacob right there in Kerala, saw that decent people nowadays were marrying, studying, working and leaving for heavenly abode from other states and other countries, yes, yes.

'You go,' he told Mira through a coughing fit brought on by speedy quaffing of warmed brandy; ice cubes could debauch even a glass of water! 'This is medicinal,' he raised his glass, ever the role model.

'So is my going,' thought she, as teary.

Mira's only sister congratulated her on her indifference to the family. 'I will do whatever is needed here. I will,' Maya grimly repeated on the eve of Mira's departure. 'Just never thought I will be the daughter who gets to sacrifice her life.'

'You are mother's pet, father's too. They won't *let* you go anywhere.'

Face in left profile for max martyrdom, Maya heaved a massive sigh. 'The point is I can't now, can I?'

With a suitcase full of ill-stitched salwar kameezes, Mira had quivered at the railway station, waiting for the Kanyakumari Express to Bangalore with all her heart. Kozhikode had everything – blue skies, soft water, kith and kin in every nook and cranny – except the unfamiliar. Who was faking a B.A. degree, who had vaginal acne...everyone knew everything about everyone. Out there somewhere was freedom, anonymity, a tattoo calling out for the nape of her neck. And men. They were going to kneel around her in a circle so that she would wear a skirt entirely made of men one day.

In the new city, she was initially too sidetracked by job-related minutiae a new breed of insolent button-bursting women at work, the pandemonium of peak-hour traffic, the unfamiliar vernacular, the eerie pop-up of her landlady's turmeric-smeared face when least expected and having to buy her own veggies to crave society. On her birthday she bought a cake, cut it and ate it all by herself. No man to share it with. But sometimes one is happy not having to share. Especially cake. Her unrequited love was wholly for the inanimate: a room she spied through a window for its symmetry or shelves, a book someone had read, the shape and ringtone of a cellphone. At nights, she lay in bed and listened to her heart thud for any of these.

Back home, her parents brainstormed with brokers and relatives to round up as many proposals as they could because, as they politely pointed out, it was mating season. Pressing a finger firmly in the air – he always rang imaginary doorbells in moments of profundity – Mr Jacob forecast marriage for her. To potter about at home seasoning sambaar for a husband, he said, simply electrified women of good breeding. He couldn't wait for his baby girls to blow up into the agreeable rubble of housewifery and labour pains and lactation and zillions of curries. 'To be loyal, supportive, adjusting and faithful is in your genes,' Mr Jacob told both his daughters equally, alluding to a long line of one-man ancestresses who embraced their lot in life, especially the marital, with feverish, high-voltage adhesiveness.

His own father had lived off a gigantic dowry by maintaining his spellbindingly ugly wife's plantations by day and painful fidelity by night. It was said the most garrulous of people fell mute for months after one glimpse of Mira's grandmother. When she passed away mid-howl in the arms of a midwife during her one and only labour pain, he promptly remarried, waving little Jacob at wedding guests as grounds for haste. The nubile new nymphet inadvertently safeguarded, despite unlimited deliveries plus a change of midwife, Mr Jacob's legacy by producing only female offspring.

'A good match,' Mr Jacob always said of his own parents. 'A good-good match.'

Each time Mrs Jacob whisked Mira into the bedroom for the sari-choosing ceremony, she'd turn lyricist on the latest suitor: 'He is a dentist/bank manager/Superman.' Sure Mira wanted her postal address to be

Ms Mira Jacob

c/o Between Two Arms

Male

but the loosely dangling hands of the eligible bachelors seemed unfit for human habitation.

'You can cook, sew and...?'

'Perform *kai-kotti-kali*,' she told them, not wanting to guarantee for all eternity the usefulness of her hands.

Nervous cough, a polite laugh. 'Hope you are not one of those women who will insist on working after the baby.'

To which she was optimistic. 'Statistically, one in 100 women dies during delivery. My grandmother did.'

Her clear disinterest in an arranged marriage devastated her parents. Up into her late teens, she had been addicted to dolls and displayed her budding nurturing skills by cutting open their plastic mouths, feeding them milk via miniature feeding bottles and scolding them when they continuously 'wet' themselves. Oh, the trouble they took to rid her of her doll-mania...'Where,' Mr and Mrs Jacob lamented jointly, separately, to each other and to everyone else, 'did all that maternal instinct go?'

A first cousin filed for divorce while an old friend fell in love.

The first cousin's husband, who had studied engineering in Switzerland on scholarships, sat behind a sofa all day 'because Saddam Hussein will come with a machine gun'. No amount of cajoling by the first cousin could allay his fears. So much so that he almost beheaded her with a sharp instrument when she attempted to move him in his sleep. Only after her neck was semi-severed thus and took up to forty stitches to rotate normal – clockwise okay, anti-clockwise okay never again – did the elders reluctantly agree to a divorce. Now the 'innocent divorcee' of future matrimonial ads twiddled thumbs at home, monosyllabic at best. 'Very sad,' as Mr Jacob summed up to Mira. 'Very-very sad.'

By contrast, the friend was full of her live-in lover. All Mira wanted to ask was about sex positions (the *Kamasutra* being so low on common sense) but what she got was: 'We both love to travel!'

Mira sniffed disapprovingly, that didn't sound sufficiently nuptial.

'Oh, he is a much better traveller than I am. I get motion-sick, tired, over-hot, over-cold, you name it. But he can walk miles, never complains, never gets sick, is never lost. You know me, I get lost outside my own front door,' said the friend, furiously downing as many masala dosas as she could for she missed them the most in the US, more than her mother she said. 'I am just thankful he takes me along…he can move so much faster on his own.'

Mira's eyes misted over. No 'He hates to eat out' or 'He can't stand me talking on the phone' to declare a man's importance, his husband-ness, his sheer power to choreograph his women. How idyllic to go away somewhere with someone only for the scenery! She still asked primly, 'What if you are just time-pass for him, you know, if he doesn't marry you?'

The friend's laugh made her mouth water. 'You know what's sadder than saying *I do* to the wrong guy? Saying *I don't* to the right. Bad girls are the new good girls, haven't you heard?'

Mira looked around. Moral or immoral, mortality rate among women was hundred percent. Who tailed couples in love till death to see what *did* do them apart? Mr Shetty, her boss, and pretty programmer Prerna Rao always left for lunch within ten minutes of each other, carefully separate up until the car park, while Mrs Shetty arranged elaborate lunches in a steel tiffin carrier that the peon carried in ceremoniously at sharp one. ('Mr Shetty has a very delicate stomach,' Mrs Shetty told Mira during a colleague's housewarming party.)

So many yes's and so many no's in so many hearts, male and female, found their corresponding matches everyday all over the world. Sometimes Mira's eyes snagged in a pair of eyes, turning her gooey and liqueur filled. Her fingers itched to run through someone's hair and her hair itched for someone's fingers to run through it. Oh, to hold hands through the day and feet through the night, ten toes curling like commas between hers! By her window in a low chair at midnight, she practised sitting in a man's lap.

No ordinary man would suit her, her man would be like this and like that. Her parents, with a pained look, resigned themselves to her bringing home riffraff off the streets. Though they equated 'love marriage' with terminal illness, they were modern enough to recognise the validity of youth in the business of breeding. Their voices faded out: 'should be a Christian', 'should have a job', 'should be a *man*'.

In due course Mira grew forlorn. Her tongue began to rise and fall in self-chat; if it happened in public she pretended to chew gum. No one died of virginity, she consoled herself, while sex killed with AIDS and whatnot. The hope that Love would eventually track her down, that the one man for whom she came gift-wrapped would locate her and tug at the satin ribbon around her and that the brick walls around her would liquefy into smothered giggles, that she would secrete solely for her soul mate and be sated till the day she died, began to flicker. The starch plain washed out of her, she was mother of heroine in cinematic terms. She grew pale and uninteresting, ate poorly and ailed deep in her heart, her hymen alone healthy as a horse. She considered her options: she could kill herself or travel abroad. But she was big-boned and the rupee too weak.

It was a tiny little pimple that did her in in the end. Which erupted red on her face like Mt. Vesuvius on a roll, announcing her pointless and useless period to a world largely indifferent to her menstrual cycle. The roses that were conspicuous by their absence in her cheeks bloomed in secret. Some flawless internal mechanism, honed by health and DNA, kept her profusely fertile, drip-dripped every month, shot sanitary napkins in the heart, leaving in its wake a sense of bereavement, of witchiness wasted, and this neon-lit acne. Right there at the corner of her mouth. She could eat it if she wanted.

For a little thing like that did she come apart. On a nondescript day like this during a depressing low-slung month, faced with a computer that did not come on at first click, it had sent her hurtling down the stairs in a tizzy into traffic jams, incoherently invoking late women of loose morals.

Wednesdays had a way of starting too early and not knowing when to stop. After her spectacular dash out of the main door, her meek return to work an hour later was stumped by a peon posted by her chair who led her, with an air of conquest, to Mr Shetty's chamber.

'I just needed some fresh air,' she said in a handcuffed voice. 'And it was almost lunch-break, sir.'

Mr Shetty surveyed her over his bifocals impatiently and superiorly. As expected, he was brimming with sense. Inflated with it. If pricked by a fingernail, he could leak logic over most of Asia for months before coming down. By and large he preferred non-marital status in his female staff – viewing uteruses as little bombs that could go off at anytime and turn into indefinite maternity leaves – but he also knew what prolonged work hours on top of chastity could do to the nerves. The last time a disheveled girl had been ushered into his office, he had been deluged with the most extraordinary rubbish about her personal life and now Mira had that same feral frank look about her that he was beginning to recognise and dread. He should hire counselors for the women around him! His own wife was as over-emotional as they come and smiled calmly only in photos, like she was doing now on his desk.

He told Mira, as if assigning her a new work project, 'Better to finish taking all the fresh air and come back...fresh tomorrow.'

Mira window-shopped the rest of the day away and at six headed home. Tried her best to shush her scootie, but too late! Hitching up her sari with its Hitler-moustache zari, her landlady came bounding down the stairs with some leftovers in a bowl for Mira. This time *vaangi bhaat* shook with the excitement of sudden transfer orders; landlady's trashcan to Mira's.

Straightaway the landlady burst into song about her husband. 'Happened just like he said. O, when it comes to TV serials, he is E is equal to MC square. He is on the phone now. Looks so angry, I didn't ask only.' And hinting at nocturnal activities that could alter power equations by dawn, she added, 'Don't worry, I will find out and tell you tomorrow.'

From the day Mira moved in, such was the steady stream of details (what breakfast He liked, His office trips, the political party He most trusted), Mira feared she was being groomed for the post of second wife in case the landlady conked off. She was a caring wife.

The husband, despite the busy world-saving schedule his wife attributed to him, always made time to stare at Mira's chest, once fixedly through wife's fifteen-minute chatter on the exact degree of tamarind in her chutneys.

The bowl suddenly fell from the landlady's hand. 'Why are you smiling like that?' she asked in a hoarse whisper.

Mira, who neither knew she was smiling nor why, stood passively by as the landlady shook her head, slowly backed up the stairs, ran into her house and shut the door firmly behind her.

Mira kicked the bowl hard then, the clang hot n' spicy in the evening air. As the stainless steel arched high against the evening sky, everything felt fictitious in a warmly possible way. 'The time is right,' she decided, 'to make my wish.' Was it too much to ask for, a man of her own? A man she could watch and watch and watch. And touch.

Give me today my daily man.

Or nightly.

She wasn't picky about the timing.

~

2

Smack! A slap woke Mira up. Still hung-over from yesterday's derangement, it took her a while to decipher where·she was, who she was and what just hit her — a birthday card sent by a sibling who sent cards earlier and earlier each year to beat postal fuck-ups.

On the card, which had bungee-jumped off the windowsill, two little Swiss girls in ballooning smocks chatted animatedly among flowers. Maya always sent her over-sweet cards in a hark-back to the childhood they never had, where sisters pssst-ed secrets and squirted perfume at each other. Mira looked at the card again: pregnant teens discussing urinary infection most likely.

Apart from the card, the room had ornamentation none. Though crystal froth and jade elephants with filigreed trunks in malls hypnotised her for hours, she did not enter the shop, fondle them, argue over their price, carry them carefully into her room and arrange them where they could catch the light. Décor she'd decide — bookshelves against pale walls or hand-woven rugs under tribal masks — only after she met her He.

Mira lay back in bed, hands under head, trying to recall the colour of her toothbrush. Blue? Red? Did she *have* a toothbrush? It gave her a kick to not brush sometimes, to carry this secret weapon in her mouth, to send a savage bad-breath 'hi' a co-worker's way…She kicked herself out of bed only to be traumatised by a sudden lack of tealeaves.

In the mirror she considered her features. God just had to do the math on her, alter flesh to bone ratio, puff lip, shrink gum, that kind of thing. The zit, she noticed, was zapped. It began to rain noisily then, as if someone in charge of her had switched on a stereo system in the sky. Later she would remember the thunder, the musk of newborn puddles, the extremely mirror-like, walk-through quality of the rain and the padded bra she wore to discipline non-seated nipples in the city's temporary winter. She tried to button up the sweater. Not happening. It was a sweater people would get up to salute. Just not her size, that's all.

Her scootie chose to go psycho. 'I will walk to work,' she threatened, but it sat there politely, not saying a thing. Unfurling a petite umbrella monogrammed 'Mira' by her mother in uneven cross-stitch – Mira's mother considered Mira's umbrellas as susceptible to theft as Mira's virtue – she stepped into the flooded road.

A short spell later Mira squelched into office with muck batiks all over her dress. In keeping with her hysterical exit yesterday, she snarled a bit, went 'aaaaagh' now and then, and pressed frantically at her jammed keyboard. Colleagues shrugged politely and stayed at least twenty inches away.

'Mi-i-i-ira, right? I noticed you are having some trouble with your source code. Can I help?' offered a total stranger with a grin so absolute she took him to be a salesman of teeth. At once aware of her hair drying inflexibly in the northwestern direction and an unbecoming slackening of the jaw, Mira mutely abdicated her chair.

'Here.' He got up after a while and then added, each word wrapped magnificently by packers and movers from his mouth straight to her ears, 'I'm Sam. Samundar Shah really but no one calls me that.' When she still gaped, as spit production had officially halted inside her mouth, he wiped his hands carelessly on his artfully crumpled linen shirt and shrugged. 'See you around.'

Though incommunicado, Mira noted a mass civil disobedience movement in her entire being: damp palms, quivering inner thighs, impaired respiration and one beating-drum heart. Flip-flop went her insides. Her navel began to tap-dance. The cursor was in spasms on the screen.

At the staff meeting that followed, Mira checked him out. From head, with hair buttered blackly to the scalp, to toe, tongue-tied in beige moccasins, he was her personal kaleidoscope for all of an hour, and she watched each of his facial features separately and raptly as if at fireworks going up in the sky. She could travel the whole world and never see a face like that again.

After the meeting, incredibly, he looked straight at her. Such merry eyes. Mira had a sudden vision of Santa lurching about blindly in the snow, eyes stolen by a Sam. 'How about lunch? I need in-house input,' he dimpled.

The keeper of the in-house input gargled violently in the loo, not trusting herself to apply petroleum jelly on lips with such shaky, shaky hands. She slapped the back of her head – more to calm her palms – and felt ready for the extraordinary event of a date. Placing one foot after the other, she reached him by and by.

'Where?' he asked, throwing her with his sudden resemblance to her mother's favourite matinee idol, Prem Nazir. The same smile. The same tilt to the head. Any minute she expected him to tap her playfully on the head and say, *mandi penne*. She-moron.

'Any…anywhere,' she stuttered, certain that he was her wishful thinking, that to onlookers it appeared as if she was cavorting with thin air.

'This is your town, you tell me. We'll go wherever your little heart desires.'

'Hmmm…' she said, for her Lilliput heart was now Gulliver and speaking Sanskrit.

Mira wasn't clued into colognes or aftershaves, but cooped up in a lift alone with him and sniffing him for the first time, she was ready to replace her oxygen. And when they sat down opposite each other in a restaurant nearby, ostensibly for the purpose of eating, she had the queer feeling they were officially turning their backs on the world.

Zigzag smiles and everything the colour of sunshine. He, who had come from Mysore and would return the day after, was deeply absorbed in all that she stammered and spoke. When her hair dangled into the menu, he tucked a runaway lock gently behind her ear, and though the part of her brain still functional knew it was meant only to unblind her, she felt the ear quietly explode.

She giggled and glittered and retained her fizz like well-corked soda, not fearing the hara-kiri moment that usually attended her social occasions. The proximity of his palm to hers on the table kept her hydrated and wondrous like the women in soap ads. But before meeting him as *the* man, she must meet him as *a* man, must steam him open.

'I love Kerala,' he gushed in a way Mira found unforgivable in others. What did people mean when they claimed to love babies/dogs/places per se? You could love a child here, a dog there, a resort somewhere, she used to think. But his 'love' was brochure-beautiful backpacker lingo and she did not go rabble-rousing into his non-specific standards. She grasped, finally, the politics of chat. If he did not keep talking her eyes would have to pack up bags and move town, she'd have to look elsewhere.

His words plopped softly on Mira like floral arrows personally twanged by fluffy *chaddi*-clad Cupids and the spicy chowmein felt like songs in her mouth. Like in a well-shaken bottle, something flowed body to brain and back, fled skyscraper mother-made strictures, rearranged microscopic neurons and heartbeat, changed her landscape. To fall in love! One fine day! In a breathless bra-tightening way!

'Am I talking too much?' she attempted a lull, made shy by his unwavering attention.

'Don't stop,' he murmured. 'I like it.'

In the evening as she readied to make a run for public transport, there was Sam, asking her how she was going home. She pointed to her feet — two of the driest, gnarled feet in the world with ten toes, uniquely and hideously, of equal length.

'They...'

She shot him a look. If he said the truth, he was a monster. If he lied, he was a monster.

'...have *character.*'

She relaxed. When asked if he could drop her home, please, her mind flitted to the matter of his inflections, how everything was made musical — a cough, a laugh, a hmmm. In the lift, they reached for the G button at the same time and Mira went *nnnnng* in the head. She felt she could shop stark naked for hours together. Or sit through ten root canals straight, without anesthetic.

En route he bought her flowers from a roadside florist. Mira let the cellophane crackle in her lap, unsurprised when it picked up the Caribbean beat inside her head. The car reached her lane, the driver parked in a side-pocket, she disembarked and they bid goodbye to each other like any other couple on the atlas. She stood there smiling very, very slightly so that her nose remained slender and any food stuck between the teeth didn't readily show. He laid his forehead on the cool glass as the car pulled out and it was very wistful, that face in the window.

She put a stool on her bed and climbed unsteadily to place the roses on the cupboard so she could see them first thing in the morning. As she drew the faded bed-sheet over her head to block traffic noises, love was no longer a word in a book or film, but a living jumping thing sitting right there on her chest squeezing the life out of her. If a faint new thump-thump thudded somewhere subterranean, she dismissed it as the anxiety of the noveau riche.

Her dreams were a haze of hyperbole. She stood between Sam and bullets in war zones and was the dying person he copiously thanked for saving his life. When Gabbar tied him to a pole, she danced on broken glass all night to secure his release.

This contentment was left largely untouched by a vicious cold the next morning. She wanted to fly to the sky and lick it dry. On her mechanic-tamed shrew of a scootie, she tilted her head to kiss every raindrop. Inside her were water lilies, lotuses and ducklings that quacked sonatas…She gazed rapturously at her office building and, feeling small and vaporous enough to be bottled like a genie, lunged towards it with lunatic joy.

Sam was in Mr Shetty's room. She watched him talk behind the glass partition. When he came out and their eyes met, it was as if a large dog licked her from inside.

'What?' he grinned, basking in her bemusement.

'Nothing…your eyes…'

'My eyes?' he prompted.

'They look different,' she blurted out.

A colleague tittered. 'From each other, you mean?' The colleague pretended to look into Sam's left eye and right eye with great care and signaled others to help her with this latest research. Unwittingly Mira had called for another roundtable conference on herself.

The morning gradually settled down to vacuous monotony and by noon even the PC looked a little dreamy. It was strange, Mira reflected, how three decades could be a blink when you met the right person. Quake-proof and suddenly, boom, 9.9 on the Richter scale. Thank the Lord it was behind her, the awfulness of waking up to the emptiness of another day, of waiting all day for night and all night for day, of jokes inside the head that made her laugh her face off but set off a spate of 'pardons?' around. Then all of a sudden, someone became the point and everything else beside the point.

At quarter to five she tripped into the loo and applied lip-gloss, a new minty flavour guaranteed to ambush male kneecaps, blotted the bridge of her nose with a tissue and shushed her hair. Holding breath slimmed her face, replaced the porcine with the angular…Mira blew a kiss at the mirror. The damsel perched on a powder-puff stool, all long legs in silk stockings, winked right back.

Sam came by at seven. 'Ready?'

She nodded happily. If she keeled over dead right now, she'd only be switching one heaven for another.

His concentration on the road as he drove could trigger only the smallest of small talk. She wanted to know his opinion of the sky, the colour of his bedroom walls, his preference in navels – pop-eyed or peek-a-boo? – but resigned herself to his abstract monologue. 'Koramangala is far,' he was saying. 'I hate black tea. The curtains in the guesthouse are thin as saris. The sunlight woke me at five. Look at that cyclist! Some people have a death wish...'

Mira drank it all in, this sporadic outpouring of existential angst, this broken soliloquy that stretched her spine voluptuously against the upholstery. Purr went her soul. He praised the city 'so lined with trees' and damned the car for its 'brainless brakes' even as Mira wanted to sing at the top of her voice something soprano about her insanity.

Table for two at a place called Rapture. Angel-hair pasta in a cheese corset with extra-virgin olive oil. Wine that strummed the tongue to hum down twin throats. A place with live jazz and blues seven nights a week, the poster for which he enthused over in great detail, especially when two men stooped to tune their saxophones in a melancholic manner. It was all her good karma in a past birth, she thought idly, chewing whatever came away on her fork. The tablemats, the napkins and the menu said Rapture on their four ends. Of course, she knew people called Joy and Jolly and Happy and Sunny, but this was the first time she occupied her own mood quite so literally.

He leaned forward during a lull in the mournful music to say, 'What do you want to do?' the words so intense they whirlpooled her head twice before settling down to make sense. He added helpfully, 'I mean *really* want to do?'

Even as Mira struggled to say something memorable – kalaripayattu on Kilimanjaro or star in a musical with him – he was saying, 'I want to paint.'

She brought every semblance of ecstasy to her face because as all women know, there are moments when you are faceless audience to a man, there only to applaud and support smilingly in keeping with the traditional portrait of womanhood hanging in an old haveli somewhere.

'I have always wanted to paint,' he told her gravely and then leaned back as if to receive her verdict – ridicule or sanction.

She couldn't, naturally, grasp the overall grandeur of his vision, but she got the gist. In the background were some people (maybe a mother or snooty ex-girlfriend) who did not think enough of this dream, of his wanting to paint, of his wanting to chuck everything in favour of something so ephemeral and hobby-ish. She would play her cards right. If they were anti, by god, she'd be pro. 'You must follow your heart,' she said with great conviction. Celestial courtesans looking in on her sighed in pride; bumbling pupils are teacher's pets. *Extol*, they cooed, *eulogise. For kiss-ass, ain't no backside big enough.*

'How do you know that?' he asked with touching humility.

Butter up, baby, chorused the courtesans. 'You,' she said with great care to jut out her lips and keep up the jut via repetition. 'You!'

'How?' he puckered up in tandem.

And they sat like that, leaning forward, eyes flailing and sinking in each other's like newborn pups thrown into sea, lips almost touching with their 'you' and 'how'.

'I...I can *see* that.'

'You can?' Suddenly he laughed a carefree, downright boyish laugh, grateful to be here with this woman. Never was blind faith more erotic. Or anti-ageing. He rubbed his arms as if the air had turned chilly.

Arms.

There was no denying it. She had a thing for arms. They made her come apart, body part by body part. Most of the time when she sat alone, she was beeping out in code: *calling all arms, calling all arms.* Forearms to be precise, elbow to wrist. She could stare nonstop, and it was a safe enough area in this country to stare at, dying to stroke and sniff. She'd seen smiling wrists on men just like she'd seen cross ones. Sometimes their elbows went straight to her knees.

He laced his fingers with hers. She pretended to check his pulse, compared palm sizes and felt for the first time the deliciousness of his hand in hers. From shoulder to fingers five, a hand all hers to hold. Maybe it was a cavewoman thing, this urge to be held and protected...

Anyway, she told herself impatiently, whatever it began with — ancestral property or arm — the whole man soon came along as attachment and one had to decide how to go about the loving. Twenty-four hours ago she'd loved him innocently, with *all* her mind, which seemed vast and bottomless enough to her, but now she licked her lips, dying to molest him, to taste the mole on the back of his...well, somewhere...he must have a mole somewhere, everybody did. Her fingers flapped under his like fledglings.

He raised their clasped hands, his mouth dead-serious against her knuckles. 'I feel urgent about you.'

'Urgent,' she echoed, 'what a beautiful, beautiful word,' and rubbed his cheek back and forth with a piss-drunk hand.

'I need a shave.'

She shook her head and left it at that though she'd have liked to clarify it was not stubble per se she liked, but *his* stubble. Stubble without him under it would only be overgrown hair poking out of the skin of somebody's cheek and she wasn't sure about that, no.

She placed her lips on his and almost jerked back. What an alien unaccustomed thing it was, another mouth. Could she convey her lust, her liking, her love, her limitations in so mundane a manner, with a mere mouth? She would have stood still as a statue for all eternity if his lips hadn't at that precise moment begun to stir.

Bluebirds flew out of her ears, daffodils sprang under her nose and all was melodious fragrance. Mira, who had never been kissed, found that a little kissing was a dangerous thing. That until the earth split open or the sky fell out, two mouths could ask for nothing more than to mash each other up.

'Come,' he said, urging her towards the car.

'Follow that man,' she told her feet.

Mira stepped into the hotel lobby with her eyes still riveted on her feet, feet suddenly so docile, so fluttery, so nautch-girl. Even his curt mutter that she walk straight by his side – and not trail behind conspicuously – to allay any suspicions failed to de-motivate her. It was just another darling bravery of Sam's.

Once she entered his room, however, it was like she exited her own body. In transit, to the she she'd be from the she she'd been put her up temporarily in the City of Nowhere. Mira felt herself grow lighter and lighter, a being briefly without weight or want. 'Don't overreact,' she shushed herself, watching him covertly as he upended his pockets on the side table. He glanced at the TV, which had come on when they entered, as if the day's headlines would decide his next course of action.

She wished she could call her US friend. She wished this so much that she caught herself inching closer to her handbag to fish out her phone. Anything would be normal compared to sitting here with a strange man waiting for sex. No saucy smile, no saucy walk, not even a saucy way to sit occurred to her. The legendary seductresses in her head had gone into exile. Mira frowned at her feet, which had propelled her here so purposefully, as if she did not know them anymore. Great, the aliens had landed and they looked like feet. She wiggled her toes; oh look, the aliens were waving back.

'Do you want to go home?' he asked, instantly comforting her with the possibility of choices. As if to get naked with him was an option just like it was to be fully dressed and halfway home.

'You don't want me here?' she asked. More amorous, less timorous.

'If I want you more, I can't zip my pants,' he said, keeping it simple.

While she appreciated the quickening of intimacy with animal ardor – he was jumping feet first into the 'them' they were only going to be – she had to squeak, 'Too much light!'

Uncoordinated by lust, he was up in a trice, to switch off the lights, twitch the curtains shut against the streetlights and flick the TV off. Then he stood where he was, waiting. She walked unsteadily towards him and when she reached him, so close that she could walk right through him and back, she hugged him. In that hug she held her heart.

Stomach to stomach they stood, very cream biscuit, till his hands grew restive at the hem of her Westside kurti. She paled a bit then and collapsed backward on his bed, no, actually the hotel bed, but his bed because he was paying the rent, or his Mysore office was. Someone was, but not her. It was not her bed, but she felt without a shadow of doubt that this was her man. Hers. And it did not cross her mind again, the ownership of the bed. It was theirs. Hers and his. And anyone else who may have occupied it, emoted in it earlier – or for that matter later – were mere tenants who had rented out the premises of their passion from them.

Her nipples, he said, were tall, dark and handsome. Soon she was the smoldering sexpot of his dreams, of her dreams, of all the smoldering sexpots' dreams. This was what it boiled down to between men and women. Pure want, the thick unassailable insoluble centre of all heterosexual urges; everything around it, the soft taffy and the caramelised candy, sucked to sweet spit. Endearments on the verge of verse, all languages left behind. Here, in a brave new world she'd always wanted to visit and now wanted to live in, a secret was born between him and her, a secret roughly their combined size.

In the morning, he ran a finger down her nose. Which reached her chin, hesitated. 'Go straight down and turn right,' she guided him to her heart.

'It is five-thirty,' he said.

She glanced at her watch, surprisingly still tied to her wrist with its glowing dial despite the fact that under that strap she had changed irrevocably. The world had calmly destroyed itself around them while they slept and he had inherited her. Swallow me, she wanted to say. I'll be your Adam's apple.

'It is five-thirty,' he repeated solemnly, 'time for me to go. I've ordered a cab for you.'

She nodded, unwilling to crawl out of the red juicy plum she had been sleeping in and supping on like a snug-smug worm.

She sat up slowly. Everything was on mute, the bed seemed to be underwater, and Sam was waiting for her to go. At the door she waved goodbye to him, the room, the unmade bed, and felt like she was bursting. She had to speak, say something, now. Now. Only happiness kept her speechless.

He said, 'I will call you', and she wanted to clap, to applaud the way their eyes met. The way only their eyes could meet surely.

3

For six months Mira thought his lie a promise. For six months, three of which had intolerably thirty-one days, she picked up her extension at first ring and spoke in a surly manner to wrong numbers and the girl who climaxed over credit cards. Six months of remembering, at the oddest moments, him on his knees between her legs, saying *five-thirty, five-thirty,* like her own personal cuckoo clock. Six months of waking up midway through the syllables of his name – 'Sa' or 'am' – to a mouth mint-fresh and intelligible first thing in the morning. Six months before people began to snigger at her do-not-disturb eyes and permanent PMS.

First month she tried, she really tried, to be busy, to distract herself, to not stare at cellphone, clock, calendar. He is taking it slow, she told herself, that's all. But even after she tended to her work and fingernails, answered mail and doorbell, boiled milk and eggs, oiled hair and scootie, flipped pages and channels, there was this surplus of her, on alert, one foot tapping, waiting.

Second month his roses drooped and shed blackish petals on her floor. She couldn't believe that while he lived on her fingertips, she did not on his. Monologuing passionately into her pillow, asking him not to come back to her, but only to explain this terrible silence, wanting to spin his no into yes, she grew desperate for an antidote to him.

Third month she felt raw and exposed, nowhere to hide. *You were too easy,* said the voices. It was love, she retorted. *But you gave it away for free, he knows what you are about. Why will he come back, for what?* For me, she whispered, but it was really a tiny whisper. She didn't want to go to work, meet anyone, certainly not visit her family back home till she grew her face back.

Fourth month she feared he had died, that his corpse was lying unclaimed in some government morgue with his mobile ringing continuously under the regulation blanket. He was, in her mind, a mass of missed calls from her.

'Mr Shah has left behind a folder,' she lied to Mr Shetty. 'I want his address to return...'

'Give it to me.' Mr Shetty grumbled, 'He's been asking for some papers I have to send anyway.'

That Mr Shah was not only alive but well enough to ask for sundry papers to be delivered to him was too much for Mira to process. When Mr Shetty came around enquiring about the mythical file, she stared at him dumbly as if he was a folksong in Tulu. And when she lied again about being mistaken on the folder altogether, only she heard the hiss of wet tears hitting her hot burning eyes.

Sam, dump me, but don't dump me now. Dump me later, much later. Please. Don't hit me where I live.

But heartbreak, she found, was on pre-paid. Vampire bats dashed against her chin and chest, searching for her vein, her neck. Derailed, denuded, deluded, deserted, demolished, damsel in distress, and that was only D. Asphyxiated, bereft, contused, egg-on-face, forgotten, gutted, hyperventilating, ill, jagged, knuckle-rapped, let down, miserable, negated, over and done with, pulped, quieted, rotting, shortchanged, tainted, unhappy, vandalised, witch-hunted, x-ed, yellowing at the edges, zonked ... her new A to Zs.

Someone scribbled inside her eyes with a red, red pen. The birthday card fell off the windowsill, hair balls slithered down the hallway, Lent followed Easter this year, it rained and stopped only to rain some more and she called herself many names, chiefly promiscuous. Her feet, she thought bitterly, may have character but she was wholly characterless.

Weekends were devoted to crying jags. The storm after the calm. Outbursts of angst and petulance against the world that pressed against her nose like a sheet of glass, outbursts to make the Mon-Sat sojourn bearable. Sundays were her day to frantically clean the toy-size flat but when a trick of lighting at sunset turned her walls to brocade she broke down all over again. She was a baby then, weak and sobbing for mommy, no trace of adult, suffering from seepage like parts of her ceiling. Crying, she found, was when all the emotional turned irrevocably physical. The pain tired of hide-and-seek and came out via the eyes and nose and mouth in deep shuddering howls as intestines hollowed and fingernails clawed at air, each organ in a separate hell. How the heart held the body hostage!

To the naked eye she looked the emotional type, but she knew better. She just hadn't seen this coming. Mornings she'd arrive at office – pride stopped her from taking days off legitimately due to her – much like before, and slump into a chair, holding her poor hyphenated heart in her hands. She barely worked, was paid just to stare at the phone. Evenings she stared out the window at home so that her face tanned evenly on a diet of aerated drinks, milk-less cornflakes and antacids. Pining. She had turned into her own mythology, Shakuntala relayed live.

'Tell me,' she interrogated herself in a straight-backed chair with the bathroom light falling full on her face and her hands tied back, 'how can I let go of that night when it was difficult enough to let go of that night on the night of that night itself?' He will spin back through that door – any door – any moment now, saying, 'so, where were we?' Won't he? *Won't he?* And she had to cope with the no-him-ness of him all over again. Get off the chair, switch off the bathroom light, lie flat on her bed and hope like hell for sleep. 'Listen,' she told him at the dead of night, 'If you are not as serious about not wanting me as I am serious about wanting you then we may just have a case, right? Let me know, please, let me know if you are open to talks on this.'

If only she could break it down to his face. Bring all her grand passion down to his face: the eyes, the lips, the nose. If it was only his face, then she could dismiss it from her mind and forget. If she forgets, she can get a lot done.

Non-negotiable glands got down to work – a nice way to call herself a nympho. Mira resented, too, the deeply private, downright clandestine, nature of her grief. If it had been cancer or a relative's death, she could mourn for all to see; she wouldn't have to be furtive, huddle in back alleys of self, wear gloves and go undercover. A fracture would mean sick leave and hospitals and sympathy and visitors with baskets of fruit, but this hairline crack in her heart had to heal on its own.

And the relentless moving forward of life and living. Of putting the washing out to dry, watching out for rogue rains. Of rounding up files wanted dead or alive at work. Of barbs from the body, replacing the whole of him with half of her hand. Of retai therapy without lists, taking untold risks in shampoos, grocerie and undergarments.

She seemed to loiter and linger and lurk all the while that sh was frantically planning elaborate trysts in the bedrooms of he mind. Detail was her joy – what he wore, what she wore, whe they cast these off, the how and what and where – though she wa stymied now and then by the solidity of walls or people going th other way. Sorry, she'd say automatically, only to find her fantas gone and her index finger hovering in midair where previously th tip of his nose had been.

Her legs grew lax and, hurried on as if by effete horsemen, h feet fell behind. She began to walk with her knees slightly splaye like she harboured gynecological secrets. She had often heard peop say FO, but never studied how someone actually fucked off. S undocumented and little-known, this act of fucking off. Now to to FO, she relied on blind instinct, on gut feeling, to go with th flow. Of FO.

She still compulsively texted and he still said nothing. D not pick up or call back, the brush-off nothing if not explicit. Th post-coitus macho silence of one who has moved on as she soug refuge in public toilets marked 'Begum', 'Stree', 'She' or 'Her'.

'I'm going to Her,' she'd announce to no one in particular a dart in to bawl.

~

30

4

While Mira cried her eyes out in a public restroom, other parts of her were on Sam's mind as he wooed his wife on the dining table of his Mumbai flat.

Delta's main assets were a bit catch-me-if-you-can, like chins you could chuck under. There was a time when they were his dim-sums, his chui-muis, his bon-bons, his cherries, his litchis...Now they were just those things on her somewhere he tweaked for formality.

Unlike Mira's monumental mammaries. Of epic proportions, cocoa-dusted, breasts he dined on, breasts that bit back...Sam shook his head. Focus, he told himself sternly; he had to apply himself to the job at hand. It had dented his ego massively when wedding night onwards all his wife wanted to laugh her way to the bank was his index finger, her fanaticism beating in the end his pet hate in positions, the missionary. She allowed variations so long she could maintain her vacation, no peasant-like toil for her. After relentlessly tying her to his bedpost week after week, Sam got over his boss complex out of sheer monotony. He also took to avoiding funerals on the off-chance that the corpse's resemblance to Delta mid-act might accidentally arouse him.

He had a nasty feeling that when it was his turn she spent her time mentally rearranging the furniture. Many times while he lay there languorous with lopsided limbs and lips, she'd declare that terra cotta was *all wrong* for the room.

'Really?' he'd ask and she would sit up enthused, entirely missing his sarcasm.

The net result was a certain flagging or preempting on his body's part, setting and perpetuating patterns where he would not beg for patience and she went woolgathering. A trip to the master bedroom induced in her immediate jetlag. And such cool eyes, when she did look back, that he was over in an instant. If she had not fallen asleep by the time he came out of the loo with freshly brushed teeth and a foolish smile, she picked up a fight. He could do no right, according to her, in the realm of romance. He, the renowned retard in the land of their bed.

Oh, when did little-girl lovers turn into women with razor tongues? In deeply personal moments, he yearned for the face she carried to those sales of hers, where surrounded by festive discounts or off-season markdowns, she came completely unhinged at the sight of bruised kettles, dysfunctional lamps and geriatric rocking chairs. Maybe if he was damaged in some way only she could identify and rectify, they could live in another marriage. He had no doubt that an infirmity, however repellent its location and nature, would bring out the Florence Nightingale in her. In a thong.

She loved him, love was not the problem, its application was. When he requested ice cream in the crotch, she deliberated long on the flavour as if dessert, not his dick, was the issue. She did what was best for him to the best of her bestness, and in all the ways she could accommodate him, she did. Which was why Sam

32

did not blow this rejection of hers out of proportion. One wasn't always in the throes of one's O's, thankfully.

When calm had been restored to his finger, Delta gave him her 'your clock starts now' look. Into twenty minutes of extended foreplay he was wondering if he should admit defeat. 'Hunnnnh,' came her indistinct mumble as she expertly dislodged him. Which was just as well. When it came to Delta, Sam found he was all dressed up only when there was nowhere to go.

When Sam and Delta got together in the summer of the new millennium in Mumbai, she had impressed him with her incredible talent for hairdos. There she'd be smiling at him from beneath a new hairstyle and it was like meeting a different girl each time. He traveled through her deep bangs to wispy fringe to beehives to laborious sides to wavelets to done-by-friend afro to wedge-cut to page-boy to bun shoved at the back to knotted round a pencil to rollers at night to tassel-straight to gelled, saliva-aided commas at the temple to pinned up high to pinned up low to pinned up neither high nor low. By the time he got past the extraordinary coiffeur, gawking at her had become a habit.

They first locked eyes at a reading of the *Mahabharata* during which she asked, with great reasoning and in old-Hindi-film falsetto, why Dushasana did not just tug off Draupadi's sari by its hem instead of laboriously pulling at a non-stop pallu. Sam instantly recognised this soul who was the very mate of his, who could involve herself with means and ends and approach issues solvingly from the other end, so to speak.

'Hello,' he said when the reading was over and everyone was sipping sour lime juice provided free at the venue.

'Hello,' she said, sounding very mid-orgasm.

'I really liked your question…' he began with disproportionate awe, still adjusting to that rare level of shrillness.

'Someone had to get Krishna all worked up and miraculous, I guess,' she shrugged. That day her hair was parted in the middle and piled up on the two sides of her head like melted horns. She replied to all his questions gravely, giving every casual query due respect, studying every angle before opining. In-depth. Analytical. Well-researched. Articulate. She was a cooking stove with all its burners on. His *Encyclopedia Britannica* turned to exactly the page he wanted.

Why her businessman father had named her Delta had been explained to him over and over again in what was obviously a rehearsed source of family entertainment. Mr Lalan who claimed to be an amateur geologist – he pronounced it 'jooljij' – said he was obsessed with deltas at the time of his only child's birth and that he had been staring at a black and white photograph of a delta when his wife's sister informed him of his fatherhood. That was all there was to the story, really a very short story, but Delta, her dad and mom, all smiled at each other so nostalgically and so lengthily that audiences felt compelled to accord her naming ceremony due sentimentality.

'So that's the story of my Delta,' he would beam.

Sam nodded respectfully each time, thinking how mirth suited most people, but not his father-in-law. The faintest smile resembled a smirk, laugh beginnings echoed distant phlegm, and the dark gums and slate teeth made the widest of grins look like someone had switched off the lights in his mouth. A power-cut kind of smile.

Mr Lalan spoke with feeling about the Plutonists who worshipped rocks as the result of vulcanism, that is, lava deposits from volcanoes, and the Neptunists who vowed rocks came out of oceans as the ocean beds dried. Plutonists and Neptunists were the mighty sword-crossed Kauravas and Pandavas with a rock for Kurukshetra. He also made realistic ocean sounds with his mouth and waved his hands animatedly, his elbows dangerously close to teacups and lesser knick-knacks resting nearby. There was a lot Sam did not know about the liquid and solid components of the planet and he showed great interest in them without looking too ingratiating or asking the same question twice because when he did Mr Lalan flew into a rage and toppled the teacups and the knick-knacks so that the liquid and solid components on the floor became a more immediate concern.

For Sam it was a tightrope walk to look educated enough to grasp geological complexities and just dumb enough to render Mr Lalan a balladeer. Having lost his own father at the tender age of ten, Sam had expected to soon dote on Mr Lalan. This expectation, unfortunately, had not borne fruit because Mr Lalan shut up shop, socially speaking, directly after the wedding.

During his first visit there as an official member of the family, Sam was astounded when not only did Mr Lalan show a certain reserve in imparting his vast knowledge about the planet's physiology but went on to actually fall asleep in his own lap! Either that or in a fit of self-respect he was contemplating touching his own feet.

As for Mrs Lalan, she continued to shower her only daughter with excessive care and attention post-marriage same as pre-, not so much excluding Sam as not including him. 'Who am I?' she was wont to ask Delta after covering the latter's eyes childishly with her hands. The fact that she did this almost on a weekly basis and sometimes in the middle of a perfectly normal conversation made Sam suspicious — maybe she really did forget who she was from time to time.

She had small eyes that involuntarily and without reason widened now and then as if witnessing private miracles. Sam soon learnt to ignore the wax and wane of her pupils and not look over his shoulder or indeed take this personally. Still, it was rather disconcerting to be talking to his mother-in-law of matters mundane, like how he forgot to buy turmeric, and have her eyes suddenly flare at him like she could see right into his soul.

But the Lalans' snub was not solely responsible for affecting Sam's innate sense of well-being. There were too many other expectations going pffft in his face.

Delta, such a keen ejector of established tastes and tradition, was disinterested in his terms of life and endearment. She took to neither his worldviews nor any shortenings of her name, however affectionate — not Dell, not Elta. Her father addressed her as Dee sometimes, but when Sam tried it she acted utterly deaf.

'Yes, doll,' he had responded when she called out once. She had come at him glowering. 'What did you call me?'

'Doll. You are, aren't you? The apple of my eye.'

'They are inanimate things, you know, doll and apple.'

He had to admit — because she asked — that while she could at one time or another be 'sweetheart', 'kishmish', 'sweety-pie' and 'phuljhadi', she would never be the tabletop, a brand of soap or Raag Darbari. 'You don't have to call me what you have already called others or have heard others call others.' She added kindly, 'That's why I have a name.'

He also found that the hair was only a part of her furious commitment to eternal change. Alterations were incessant and the only constant was variation in terms of interiors and her own personal exteriors. Her hair, her laugh, the décor of their loo were all subject to amendment without notice and if he knew where he was and with whom, it was only because he was on the lookout for these things. He was not surprised when the towel that hung on a hand-painted nail one day dangled down a headless voodoo toy the next. When they retired to bed at night, pleasantly tired by the preceding day, he knew that inside her head resting on the pillow was a plot to upend the next day as best she could.

She had giddied him in the initial days. Doing her surya namaskars in the evenings: 'Why bring the sun into stretching exercises?' Shaving off her mane, gaining an ascetic aura that got Sam all worked up. After changing the subject for days when he came on to her, she wanted to do it on the windowsill. He refused — no amount of foreplay could blank out the fact that they lived on the sixth floor — even as he tried to shift her kinkiness to the safety of his bed. In his perplexity, he frequently overstated while referring to her, a fact that his mother, Leela-ben, rarely appreciated.

Delta was his wife, and, yes, she was a slim young thing without the trademark Gujju hips, agreed Leela-ben, and then implied without saying a single word, and pray, of what use was she and to whom. To her, Delta was a spoilt brat, a daughter brought up as son, and the one time their differences had blown up into a confrontation, Leela-ben had exclaimed loud and clear, 'You are a man!' which was the worst insult known to Leela-ben's ilk but had Delta looking touched for days.

Leela-ben did not belong to the new breed of track-suited mothers-in-law despite Delta's westernised sing-song of 'mom' and Sam's following suit by deserting the more down-market 'ma'. Leela-ben had been a young bride, young daughter-in-law, young mother and young widow, and recovered really from none of these. Also, there had been the earthquake that rumbled fiercely and fatally through Gujarat the year Sam and Delta got hitched.

The quake had only been the beginning. Straight off it killed eight of her neighbours (all new-money types but still!), smithereened all her belongings and buried her in silt for ten hours straight. Though TV channels and local politicians made much of her after she came out of the rubble, she was just grateful for the rebirth. Gujarat, she knew, had gone through so much more after she ran out in a hurry that day, leaving her shattered home behind and pretending to do so only to please her son when in reality she had felt so vacuumed out, so hollow, so much husk. A city must lay its foundations right and map out its canals and sewers and pillars as strapping as can be, if it wants citizens that is.

It had been a matter of letting Sam pack some clothes, some jewelry, rescuing photographs of the Shah family from albums of others (for tangible proof of their existence before the earthquake), take those few steps to the tarmac and plane, seeking another permanent address.

The hours that Leela-ben spent under her own house, convulsed by after-shocks, convinced her of one thing – that practicality and a brain that could tick efficiently under stress were the only two virtues worth possessing. Her son, she readily admitted, had neither. Now if only his wife had either...

Despite the fact that Delta was from the same community, Leela-ben could not bring herself to do a wholehearted *dandiya* at their wedding. Not while her daughter-in-law maniacally rotated those nonexistent hips of hers with C-section written all over them. Forget babies, could she manage an average bowel movement was what Leela-ben wanted to know.

Uncaring of her mother-in-law's disapproval of her carefully cultivated boho chic, Delta continued to haggle over antique chests with brass knobs in rundown homesteads or flea markets and then sell them for double the price at high-end boutiques. The addresses of these families were furnished by Leela-ben who, courtesy her hometown trips at least six times a year, was in a position to wangle such sales. They were unlikely work partners and the extent of the older woman's remuneration began and ended with an annual tussar silk sari or a quilt salvaged from old clothes by some malnourished tribal girl that Delta packed with such ethnic pizzazz each time. Leela-ben would murmur, 'you shouldn't have', and worry what this chit of a girl would do if the world suddenly collapsed around her ears.

No, Delta couldn't suck up to Leela-ben. Not without her uterus. Only a baby could bring the two together. The commercial manufacture of Viagra did bring a sparkle to Leela-ben's eye as she had come to accept the grim possibility of reproductory apparatus being faulty closer home.

Whenever she spent the night at their place, they never shut the bedroom door and, much to her discomfort, conversed with her through the night with the lights on. And post-quake Leela-ben did overvalue light – both natural and unnatural. At nights she demanded that the brightest light be kept on and Sam understood his mother's need for light. A window was left open in her room and an oxygen mask hooked to the wall but she still craved larger nostrils to suck up all the oxygen she could...But Sam and his wife happily keeping their lamps lit and door open spelt only one thing to Leela-ben – No Sex.

One overcast day Leela-ben could bear it no longer. 'Do you have sex with your wife?' she asked her son, looking him in the eye as by now the question was a constant drumming in her blood and beyond genteel reference.

He stammered, 'Yy...yes. Sometimes. Weekends. Holidays. Nights when we both don't have to get up early the next day.'

'When was the last time you did it, son?'

'At her parents' place, in her old bedroom, on an orange mirror-work bedspread now that you ask, mom.'

'But are you doing it right?'

'What do you mean *right*?'

Here Leela-ben pretended some sheepishness. 'I mean,' she said with downcast eyes, 'is the baby-juice going into her baby-maker?'

'Yes,' he said hurriedly.

'Does she sleep with her feet up on a pillow afterwards?'

Compelled to relive the role of his hand in the proceedings, Sam felt his index finger tic. Damn his smothering mother. She loved someone, straightaway she was the pillow on their face. 'Listen,' he promised her on an impulse, 'you must pray. God is sure to give you grandkids.'

Following the discomfort that both parties suffered from this conversation, Leela-ben decided to retire from maternal prodding for a while. One look at Delta and even she understood the difficulties of mounting the woman. Nothing good could come out of girls wearing pants, smoking, drinking, swearing, cutting off hair, or boys shaving off moustache, piercing ears, tying ponytails etc. All this ardhanari business did not bode well for the next generation, if indeed there was to be a next generation! Men, in her opinion, needed to be men. And with a wife who'd been brought up like a boy ('We never let Delta enter the kitchen!' Delta's silly mother bragged), her Sam was frilling at the hem.

Unknown to her, Sam too worried over losing his masculinity. Until a real baby came along, he knew he was destined to be babied by both mother and wife. He needed a smaller, weaker male around to appear macho by comparison, and shift him from Plant Kingdom to Animal Kingdom. But many were the hitch. Despite Delta's fervent declaration of wanting a baby, she was not working towards it in any biologically recognised way.

Fortified by Leela-ben's recent enquiry and some erotic literature he chanced upon, Sam confronted his wife on the subject of intercourse. He almost quailed when her eyebrows peaked and eyes narrowed. But with the invocation of the magic word – children – Sam was able to enlighten his wife on the need for some old-fashioned nookie. Really, when had she gotten so out of hand? And when would she get off *his* hand?

One thought led to another as it often does and he caught himself idly wondering if it could be different with another, er, party. The minute The Third entered his imagination, it was well-nigh impossible to expel it. At first Sam was confused as to the exact gender of this party. A couple of men had poked him playfully in the ribs and winked about his babe of a wife, and he had panicked;

41

a cool guy and a hot chick, they should make room temperature at least. No boyfriends for him, he made up his mind after standing too close to one or two men. His physical reaction to non-Delta women, however, left nothing ambiguous. Bring on the dancing girls, he hollered, the item girl!

Fleshed out on a regular diet of sinful magazines and the sight of ordinary women going about their business, Sam began to fantasise. Positively obese in certain areas, his playmate held her own against gravity only because she was imaginary. And though he adored her indistinct facial features and the blinding full-on smile, he had to admit that consummation was a problem. Getting a US-made full-size plastic doll with a cunt that gave off electric shocks did occur to him, but where would he keep the damn thing? He would have to rent a place for his 'mistress' and employ a human housekeeper who'd nicely goof off in the absence of a real memsa'ab which would mirror his current life to such an extent that one day he would end up giving the doll a hand-job.

He dreamt of leashing women, live women, by long, long plaits and often excused himself to the nearest loo. So ready to try a new love, the furtive, fugitive kind, but first he had to overturn his old notions of love, chain the clingy, nagging him and liberate the Don Juans in him. His lips twisted funny, he felt wicked, he wanted to pillage, to plunder, to sodomise life so far. And though all these plans nearly palsied him with pleasure, he knew instinctively that discretion was the better part of valour.

Sam briefly toyed with the idea of taking family friend and newly-single Stuti's mild flirtation to a tangible sphere but balked at Delta's possible discovery of such a transgression and subsequent hysterics (at best) or divorce papers (at worst). It all came down to a matter of space finally – him, her and a soundproof room. Where? Where could he take a likely lay? When it was just your body and hers and real estate was a bed somewhere...

He began to look, really look, at women. Going beyond their helloes to visually compute their vital stats. After he had stared at his colleague Kusum chewing a pencil tip with more relish than warranted, the women at his workplace started to adjust their dupatta more decorously around him. Matters came to a head when his senior – a pulao-raita ex-PSU type – called him in and asked him if everything was all right.

'Yes, it is,' Sam stated firmly, because things were finally all right for him. He was going to have his cake and eat it too like everyone else.

'You seem...distracted,' said the senior.

In the ensuing conversation, Sam learnt that two women had complained about him making inappropriate eye contact, and that Kusum, traumatised against both pencil and pen, could now only type and that too erratically. Immediately Sam babbled about the lack of babies in his life and on his lap and the ensuing mental mayhem. His unconvinced senior, who only wanted the matter to be put behind them pronto, suggested to Sam an outstation trip just long enough for everyone concerned to forget 'this little unpleasantness'.

Almost being called a perv took its toll on Sam, but in an unexpected way. He knew, and he knew this well, that until and unless he got some tail, he would always, always ogle ineffectually at the world. Only action could satiate him all the way up to his eyes.

43

The complainants accorded him a halfhearted farewell and went back to wearing sleeveless after his departure and the lone co-worker who took him to be bug-eyed from a thyroid problem did not spare him another thought.

~

5

Mira collected four items of clothing and made for the trial room. The tiny cubicle, replete with three full-size mirrors, was lit up like a Christmas tree. She threw the clothes into a corner where they lay jumbled and pliant against each other, and sat on the small black leather-padded stool. She covered her face with her palms and took a deep breath. She removed her hands from her face and looked into one of the mirrors: she looked so different, so timid and so submissive, like those clothes in the corner, new but creased, unused but already soiled.

And these age spots, she looked closely at her upper cheek, had rained down from nowhere. They were not hers, she disowned them, would never reconcile to them, but did they care? She peered closer, at her eyes, her *starving* eyes. Yes, they were the ones acting all wonky. She knew what they were famished for. Not everyday sights, not her own face staring back, not this air-conditioned cubicle with its discreet Mozart, but a man and not just any man but *him*!

She watched herself stealthily, terrified of the candor in her face. Under these bright lights, with the mirrors returning your eyes threefold wherever you looked, sitting around just...wanting did not seem right. She lowered her eyes. She couldn't take such honesty in her own eyes.

Slowly she stood up, peeled off her blouse, hung it on the hook behind the door. And then she thought, what if this was his room, his bedroom, the room he slept in and her hands suddenly stilled, lazing on her skirt. She teased the elastic waistband down and then unhooked her bra and shrugged it off her shoulders with picture-book élan. When she looked into the mirror again, she looked…sleepy. Narcotic.

She reached out for the orphan clothes lying in the corner to give them a home on her body. The floral chiffon floating loose, the tights ready to kiss her calves, the black beaded top with the scooped out back and the peach camisole fluttering like a cool breeze. These of course were not her type of clothes but she was rapidly filling up her cupboard with just such nonsense.

She had longed for someone vaguely like Sam for so long and she had longed for a speech carefully chosen for her, aimed solely at her ears with words so tender, their backs broke as they surrendered their meaning. She had longed vaguely and now she longed with a focused longing – the intensity fairly unseating her. So curious about all things him. The sugar in his coffee, how he would say certain words, his preference in shirts (stripes/checks/plain), if seafood agreed with him, would he laugh at this or that, was he breastfed. Naively, she had told him, this man, of all her longings and he had just *gone*. It all came back to her then – disappearing dolls, the absent bridegroom, beautiful sister, the biological clock, the boredom, her empty bed…She *had* to leave, he had already waved farewell. All that was left was to smile politely and say OK then, see you sometime, no, no, I have my own transport. Back to my own life.

Mira sat back on the stool with a thump, jarring her spine. All her knowledges weighed heavily on her. She had been asked to adjust here, in the deepest places in her heart…It was not a perfect world outside of her head. Inside her head was a crooked grin, an inclined head, poetry and an unlined heart. Inside her head was an oasis of him and her and fingers linked so long so strong they'd fossilise eventually for some future archaeologist. Inside her head was total crap.

Mira opened her eyes. To the garish lights and the floral top, which she briskly tried, decided against and prepared to walk out. Don't misbehave, she begged the mirror. We have to get out, face the day, the chores, the officing, the weeks, the months, the years, a whole lifetime. Her shoulders sagged. She can't do it. Not like this. Not alone…OK, OK, she told herself. That's enough, first things first. She had to unclick the latch, exit the cubicle, the shop, in that order.

Three out of four, the shop assistant muttered, taking the fourth and tossing it into an enameled bin meant for rejected clothing. Mira paid for the three she took, said her thanks to the billing clerk and limped into the sunny outside world. She thought, now if I can just cross the road to my scootie, I will be any woman in the world driving herself home.

The landlady's husband made an enigmatic entry into her house that weekend.

He cleared his throat. 'The landlady,' he said, referring to his wife in keeping with how she always referred to herself, 'is gone to her mother's home in Chikpet.'

Mira broke into polite questions about the health of the landlady's mother, the landlady's return etc, carefully inserting 'sir' in every sentence.

He brushed her queries aside. 'I am alone,' he paused. 'You are alone.'

A piano crashed through the ceiling of her skull. Ah, Sam the Second. Less sophisticated, more piecemeal, but definitely Sam-like with his touching faith in female libido. She went through the routine denial, anger, sorrow in a split second this time. She got it now, this flattering attention from a member of the opposite sex. Its momentary might, its volatile hello, its lack of spine, its loose ends flapping in the air. Not for nothing had Sam happened to her.

'The landlady must never know, sir,' she said softly.

He shook his head so hard, it squeaked on its hinges. She had taken the words out of his own mouth. No, no, never tell the landlady.

'The landlady must never know, sir,' continued Mira, 'about my operation.'

Wildly hopeful about birth control being taken care of, he still had to ask, 'Operation?'

'I was born boy but inside I was girl, *that* operation, sir. Now only last touch-up needed. But almost you can say I am like full girl.'

'Sir' staggered back.

'Remember not to tell landlady,' Mira called out thoughtfully. 'She will want to know how you know this, sir.'

~

6

'I have a confession to make,' Sam said.

Delta, who was trimming her sideburns into pointy ends so they'd stick out like spears from under her beret, stilled the pair of scissors and scolded, 'Donx!'

This abbreviation for Donkey was what she called him to indicate affection, intellectual superiority, ownership and occasional horniness. As per her own orders, it was neither inanimate nor overused. Also, it kind of went with her name, the alliteration. Delta & Donx. 'Sweet na?' she had asked him during the good old days when she used to ask him such things.

'I...Delta, don't get mad. Promise me first that you won't get mad,' he said urgently, avoiding her eyes, which were armed with kohl on lower eyelid, eyeliner on upper eyelid, mascara on every eyelash and dissent. She looked, as always, flammable.

'There you go applying for anticipatory bail!'

Sam did not care for the disdain in Delta's voice. Having been away for a while, to Mysore, Bangalore etc, and having therefore forgotten her brutal way with words, he felt a little sensitive these days. When she did not prompt him to complete his sentence, he said, 'I am thinking, only *thinking*, mind you, of…' He looked at her guiltily.

'Of?' she wailed in G Minor. It wasn't her fault, inborn nasal aggravation ensured high octaves at all times.

His own voice sank to the ocean-bed. 'Going back to my painting.'

Delta moaned at him, her better half. Following that accidental meeting of eyes, the *connect* and the conspiracy of hormones, key family members and auspicious dates in their horoscopes.

'Are you unwell?' he asked, concerned.

Exactly what she wanted to ask him! She threw the scissors on the floor and walked out of the room, hoping her diva act would put paid to his arty nonsense. Theirs was a humanitarian marriage, with more fresh air than love. But charity, which had begun at home with her putting up several prime examples of Sam-signed ugliness on her handsome walls, couldn't go on indefinitely.

Sam picked up the scissors, whistling. His wife was temperamental, true, but he was the gifted one. It had only taken a spot of studding in the South to unearth it all over again. When his office shunted him out on tenuous, unsubstantiated charges of lechery, at first he had sulked. Then the particulars of the move consumed his waking hours, and after many a mushy speech, chiefly the reiteration of their wedding vows in a coochie-coo version with Delta, Sam had been a free man. Not for long though. His predecessor had left the Mysore office in a mess and it took all his mind and MBA to straighten it somewhat.

The streets of the city were paved with PYTs. College girls and colleagues went about their lives, leaving him cross-eyed, delusional and in a state of constant arousal. A young girl would be ideal for frolic, he decided. They could not *compare*, were eager for attention, and, if subordinates at work, just poor enough to impress. There was, in particular, that trainee who shook her ponytail at him beguilingly, all saucy scrunchies. But again, he argued, older women knew the score, would melt back into their marriages without a murmur. Bored housewives pathetically grateful to lift their petticoats...

He awaited orgies, threesomes, woman on woman, all that the internet promised and more. The wives of his managers and staff, however, had never read porn, at least not his collection, where they were supposed to accost him with slipshod skirts, ready to do anything – sir, *anything* – for their husbands' promotion.

His hard-on, meanwhile, took up permanent residence in his pants, till he feared that only an amputation would end such eternal tumescence. He had once clutched Lily the trainee to his chest on the pretence of horseplay, but she smelt a bit off, of some semolina breakfast and a peculiar southern soap. A dalliance with her was not off-limits, in fact was thoroughly possible, but the damage to his wet dreams, not to mention his nose, would be incalculable. No, she won't do. In the interim he rehearsed Santa-Banta jokes to go with rava idlis.

Not an iota of guilt cramped his style. Like most married men, he focused less on the said sacrifices or adjustments by spouse and more on instances of direct disloyalty. Why couldn't, for instance, Delta cook for him? Why must some smelly, unhygienic stranger manhandle his meals day after day? Didn't his mother drop everything just to make his little evening snack when he was a schoolboy? Why, Delta even thought he was faking lactose intolerance. When his stomach seized up, she always looked surprised.

He was in love with 'next, please' precisely because the new faceless, formless female had never said 'no' to him in the way that his wife already had and could never take back or undo. On the one hand was Delta's so-called love for him. On the other hand was his hand, tired and ready for a holiday.

As far as Sam was concerned, the planned affair had stopped denoting merely the sexual and had become an anthem for freedom along the way, for life as he had previously lived it, for innocent pleasure and feather-tickling of mind, in short, for bachelorhood once more – this time knowing it for the luxury it really was. He had to rectify his lifetime regret of marrying too young. He had to get off.

But where, oh, where was his soul-mate of the here and now? He hadn't come all the way to Mysore to jerk off. Not that to masturbate in such sylvan surroundings was a hardship, but he had come in search of 38C. Real, living, breathing 38C that spilled over in drunken helloes.

Then came the Bangalore trip, an olive branch extended from heaven itself. Staring at the sky from his miniscule guesthouse balcony on the eve of his departure, Sam hummed an old love-song, gulped down his rum-coke and threw his fists in the air – *dishum, dishum* – to prepare for the latest episode of his life. A swan song for all his stale unused sperms so that when he 'made love' to Delta, he'd manufacture one hell of a perfect baby with fresh stuff. For that had been Delta's teaser whisper to him: 'Donx, let's make a baby when you come back.'

Two days. He had only two days, Sam kept reminding himself, before he went back to his own life. After the Bangalore trip, he was to return to Mumbai, to his Ghatkopar home and cold-fish wife to whom he had touchingly gifted his virginity five years ago in a flower-bedecked bed with loud film music playing on the speakers from the windows as Mr Lalan had paid for the whole night and that meant the whole night dammit even if he went deaf in the process.

The morning of his arrival at the candy-striped office in Bangalore kept him guessing. And then he saw her! Or rather he saw her rain-drenched upper half as she strained her eyes at the monitor before her. Even before he heard her voice, even before she met his eyes, even before he could introduce himself to her, he wanted to ooze gently on her thigh.

The intense overhead bulb and the PC's beam irradiated Mira's blouse to such luminosity that her bosom seemed to catch fire right before his eyes. Her positioning, her backing of the fancy blinds, the potted plant along her left, all caused the screen's light to fall directly on her chest and face – the radiance that pulled Sam to her like the idiot man in fairness ads suffering from terminal racism.

Of course, the rest of her followed the full-cream rack: the bed-head, the chewy corners of two lava lips, the unpremeditated attire, the subservient smile, the glimmer of hero-worship and the hula-hoop walk off an oversized derrière.

He asked someone, 'Who is that?'

And that person had replied, Miss Mira, leaving him in those first five unguarded vital minutes to mistakenly absorb honorific as first name and by the time reality registered, he had been smitten. Sold to the pair of boobs in the first row.

Her spinster status, when it dawned, brought on no scruples. Sooo, he drawled mentally, not married, but the reasons for staking someone's spouse were secondary to Mira's potential virginity and the intoxicating unlikelihood of comparisons.

Sam sighed, back in his uni-dimensional, single-entendre, monochrome world, as his wife walked back into the room. 'Look at me, Donx,' she ordered, taking the scissors from his hand.

He had no choice but to look her in the eye while his tailbone still trembled like a tuning fork in memory of Mira's more tender ministrations.

'You do know you are a grown man with responsibilities. I don't have to tell you...' Suddenly the Airtel jingle was upon them. 'Stay right here,' she ordered him, and walked into the balcony, where the network was better.

Sam stayed exactly where he was. Meeting someone's eyes was a huge responsibility. Meet an eye and it instantly demands honesty, empathy, secrets. You can't for the life of you remember any other eyes at the time. It is like you owe your eyes to these eyes. Your eyes exist in another pair of eyes, you are aware of only this. You see things the way these eyes see things and forget this is temporary. That another pair would demand another loyalty from you.

Meeting Mira that first time, lunching with her, dropping her home he'd been in purgatory-paradise. She acquiesced, and heavy breathing followed. His desperation, his neediness and his anticipation (unconsciously from wedding day onwards and consciously from Mysore-trip onwards) turned sex into a blow to the head. He had been concussed, yes that was it. And what was a little preemie ejaculation between two people who'd just met?

Late next afternoon he was with his wife who welcomed him with open arms. In the night her legs followed suit. 'Donx, Donx,' she kept repeating against his jaw, neck, chest and, well, everywhere, as Donx had originally been her abbreviation for *that*!

'Donx!' she cried now, back from the balcony, her manner about-turned and face already outdoor. 'I have to go out. I'll be late, you go to sleep, okay? And order something to eat.'

Sam did not reply, uncaring that silent treatments needed a listener.

7

She had hard-core fantasies about his death. Something inexplicable and bulky coming down on him, like his roof. Face crushed but incandescent under the chandelier. Succumbing to venereal disease, so new, so fatal, they'd name it after him. Fed so much poison, his pee was India's leading export in pesticides.

Cradling Sam's dying head on her lap would be her convalescence. Mira smiled thinly, only to stop smiling. Movement, even the smallest, carried a statutory warning about injuries. Her heart had grown bristles. Each time she breathed, they poked the insides of her chest. It was undoubtedly a time of pain, pain puréed into its very essence.

It is only when hearts break that one thinks of the raw materials that make up a heart. Her thoracic region throbbed, her tongue flopped like a dog's on a hot summer day, her nostrils flared for no reason in the middle of the day, she buzzed and buzzed non-stop, irritating herself in the ear like an ingrown mosquito. Worse, she couldn't shoo herself away. Her periods punched her harder in the stomach, aches stapled her joints, sunshine stung her eye, squeezed her temple and evaporated her tongue, even water scarred her mouth.

Falling in love had aged her. Rejection was why, Mira realised belatedly, some of her colleagues had that weather-beaten, hard-eyed, *used* look. That was how the rebuffed half coped, by closing down their face, those parts of it that gave away secrets. The day before she met Sam, she'd been young, with the world to anticipate, with nothing to hide, with lots of things to laugh about and now, wham, she was an old hag. Crow's feet ran down her cheeks and her black hair grew white highlights. She remembered picking a strand of her hair off him. Curled long and black against the detergent blue of his T-shirt.

A woman with a past, she had become that.

So she teetered between 'us' and 'I' and 'him' and 'them', between specific hungers and general gluttony, between Googling vasheekaran mantras and the sheer craziness of third-personing herself. It all got very intolerable till she lost her temper. Of course, implosions were routine, but explosions somewhat new.

'Yes,' she screamed down someone at work, 'I am a fool. I am your basic A-level fool. Stand next to me for instant upgrade. I make anyone look good!'

The other girl scurried away with her hands up in mock surrender, pretending to be a poor little thing.

Still, her outburst was the talk of the office and for hours afterwards, it elicited comment around the coffee-machine. Mira was aware of the covert glances, the almost-awe she had inspired. A watermelon had once burst of ripeness in her house and its sweetness and seeds had scattered into a distance. There was the sound of a gunshot – bam! – and the most inaccessible of corners were sprayed with fruit. You can't be too full of anything, not even sweetness, it would seem.

Mira was back at the church, one day with accusations, another with apologies, yet another pleading for him back in her life and another begging for plain and simple sleep, so tired was she. Away from the church, she settled for gross distrust in self. For if she had been pleading for beauty, it was presumed she had brains to begin with. And that was where she hurt most, inside her skull – migraining was what her head did best these days – for it was her brain that betrayed her with its lack of judgment and discretion, and now she stood exposed as the ugly idiot with neither intelligence nor looks. Falling in love with a stranger was such specific stupidity, it did not bear thinking about. What had she known about him except that he looked like that or spoke like this, what he wore and the colour of his socks and eyes? Women like her, living alone by their wits, had to keep it together at all times, had to be *sensible* till they die!

The final tears that came gushing out of her had her repeatedly whimper 'I'm sorry I'm sorry' to herself. And she *was*, sorry that she had put herself through this cycle of hope and hopelessness, of the injustice she had meted out so carelessly to self. But that was absolutely the last tear shed on the subject though she remained soft and bruised long after.

She even got sentimental about her family, went so far as to dial Maya's mobile one silly Sunday. Not once but thrice. She couldn't blame her sister for not picking up. Turning to the window once again, Mira inhaled deeply. Then she took another deep breath, chin down, sniffing herself. Heartbreak? Gravy?

Nine at night the phone rang. Village calling the idiot back.

'Mira, what happened?'

58

Mira brushed away the belated enquiry. 'Nothing,' she said, 'Not a thing.'

A second before nine she had thought it possible to move on, to put the past behind her, that she had legitimately cried her way out of it. Between the dizzying heights and the doldrums, a desired domicile called Survival. Recounting would have brought it all back – the explanation of the bliss (necessary to justify the immensity of the error), his shallowness (with footnotes on surface charms), her anguish (directly proportional to her stupidity)...What had happened was a mere chronology of events, an accident of two lonelinesses crashing into each other with no witnesses except the victims. Besides, Maya would demand proof, of the deflowering, of the feelings in her heart, of the treachery, of the pain, and then she would turn her in for thirty silver coins, Judas that she was.

'Amma wants to know if you are using the umbrella when you go out in the sun.'

'Yes, yes, I am,' Mira replied automatically. No tragedy worse than a tan for girls!

Maya sighed virtuously into the phone and hung up.

The tattletale. When Mira had been banned from playing with dolls, Maya would sneak into the room while Mira was twisting the sheet into a round head with the rest of the sheet the flapping body, catch her 'red-handed' and make such a ruckus. Maya had stabbed her dolls with little scissors – their eyes, their necks. 'It is plastic,' she would say when Mira managed to catch hold of her and slap. Plastic. Now she would examine Mira's heart and declare it plastic too.

Mira remembered complaining to her mother that Maya was hiding her dolls, decapitating them, forking out their eyes with the compass in her geometry box. And her mother had said, no, no, don't put each and every blame on Maya. But Mira, taking no chances, had whacked Maya hard, just in case.

Mira emptied bowls of candied cherries, bought a roadside book on combating depression, watched the butcher chop plump animal limbs into bite-size pieces, and gradually steadied her pulse rate. It was all right, she told herself. It was just a matter of...

Time Vs. Right Now

Head Vs. heart

Self-help books Vs. chick-lit

See, all neat and tidy, in separate don'tmatchthefollowing sections. Just draw the line hard between them with a 2B pencil. No more inside out, upside down, head over heels. Once she had grasped the truth – every dog may have its day but every day has its dog – there was no mistaking her determination to heal. With the gilt of chocolate wrappers crackling under her feet, she wallowed in home truths. She had to care for him two hoots:

1. Hoot.

2. Hoot.

Though she had known that exactly this degree of loneliness awaited her, it was the brusqueness of the bestowal that scrambled her so. In the distant future, she had seen her love shred to potpourri in the mind, gently perfuming her sighs, rendering her subtly older and wiser, because every man and woman can't be moth to flame. She had imagined one setting sun, two hands slowly de-linking, four bitten lips as they bid goodbye with Band-aid on their hearts because, well, because men like him did not end up with girls like her, not if they wanted to carry the race forward.

She continued to text on auto-pilot for another week. Once at two a.m. 'Yours till i die'. Historically enough, for the very first time, there actually came a reply, but a reply that maimed and minced and imprinted itself on her bone marrow. It merely asked, as if her own message had implied no innuendoes, 'Who?'

She reared back as if stung. Like she had opened a door and caught him in bed with another woman. She wanted to kill. Oh, how she wanted to kill the man who said look into my eyes and then looked at some other woman. Keep breathing, she told herself, keep breathing. A week later she texted, 'Me. Mira'.

Um, change the order please, 'table for two' to a 'coffin for one'. Pollyanna died. The police just called. Head-on collision. Didn't feel a thing.

Briefly she considered letting go of the crazies and making do with Iodex or some such balm. But to be so *forgotten* and so *quickly* was inexcusable. Being fobbed off, by and large, was not what she objected to, it was not being consulted. She had pictured glass jars vying for his brain after his death and the man couldn't come up with a more polite 'Piss Off' to her? When the little affair – she called it that though she was aware that perhaps the technical name for what they did was something else from another dictionary between men and women that she had no access to right away – unfolded, she had been an equal player in it. Managing to meet eyes, shy then bold. They had been together, in step. Now she was revealed standing alone in the spotlight for having taken further steps in her dirty little mind...By withdrawing wordlessly, he had sprung hierarchy upon them.

You want out, come say it to my face.

Shinie Antony

No, it was not the delinking, abrupt or otherwise, that disturbed her so. It was the brutal dismissal of her as a person, an equal party, a decision-maker. Did he think he could erase her by switching off a bloody phone? As if she'd been a roll in the hay, a bit on the side, his piece of fluff, a good-time girl, a fling, finger food, amuse-bouche, an appetiser, a – she had to whisper this even to herself – *one-night stand*. But where do you report the loss of an unsung hymen? A lifetime of innocence and trust and sweet hope in one size that fits all?

Mira looked down at the T-shirt she wore, the one her US friend had given her. Go forth and multiply, it said in big block letters, Noah's signature tune now slang for 'get lost'. *I'm going, I'm going, but.* How long is one to just ache?

She consulted God.

God helps those, said God in a cunning third-person voice, who help themselves.

~

62

8

Mira was still clueless when the Shettys went on a holiday to South Africa. During his absence Prerna came in with red-rimmed eyes and announced she was working out her notice period. Everyone exulted at the scent of a scandalette and debated the why and how as long as they could. Prerna, it was suspected, let slip some detail to Mrs Shetty that brought the latter's tiffin transmissions to a grinding halt. South Africa was apparently an attempt at appeasement rather than a romantic overture on Mr Shetty's part. And though conservative murmurs were all for Mrs Shetty's perseverance and ultimate marital win, unsaid praise was reserved for Prerna's spunk. While Mrs Shetty briefly got another continent, Prerna had pulled off Mr Shetty's pants!

Balancing a sheaf of papers in the office's narrow-hipped corridor, Mira concretely began to dream of her own retribution. It was born when a gaggle of girls, all uber-hep, fell silent at the sight of her. The sum total of all hatreds – for her holier-than-thou sister, for the classmate who got engaged to the boy of her choice, for the friend ferociously lusted after in different locales, for the supermodel colleagues who tricked her into calling Mr Shetty Mr Shitty on her first day at work, for Sam, her Sam who was really not her Sam but his own Sam who upped and away-ed from her precisely because she was a wimp of the first order, and for herself who couldn't wait to *fall in love* – was now officially a full-blown terrorist attack in her basement.

All the bad-girl ghosts began to jump up and down inside her, pouty and petulant, stamping their spiky stilettos, baying for blood. Mira addressed them first of all: 'Scram, girlie ghouls!'

Geishas froze, full of grace. Sirens got sore throats, averting shipwrecks, letting all the pretty sailor boys get away. Zombies plunged back into the warm wormy earth, lap dancers scrambled off male laps and yelped for mommy laps, yakshis could hold a tune no more. The orchestra grew muted, swelled one last time, hushed forever. Only the banshees wailed.

Crumpets and strumpets, hussies and harpies, not bashful anymore but deeply diabolical monkeys full of mischief. Floozies and slags counting all their money; there was no pleasure in prostituting slammed against a grimy wall without this jingle and this jangle. Hookers, beware, hard cash instead of the stupid, stupid heart every time. Baring claws and maw, twitching a serpentine tongue, the bitch blew her nose.

It was on a full-moon night that every drop of Mira's blood turned werewolf. Hate, like love once had, arrived unconditional. Hate, love – no one slogged for these. It was just there, bam. Like calcium deficiency. Or a blood group.

In her first act of anarchy 'Sam' became 'Littleshit' on her phone. She practiced witchcraft on cacti. *I wish you dead. I wish that six months from now someone will tell me you died on this day, this hour.* Women may have meant him harm before, but she had something they all lacked: a black tongue. She opened her mouth, stuck out her tongue – aaaaah. Nice and black. OK, she amended. Let's begin small. She wished him itchy scalp, falling hair and lots and lots of dandruff. She smiled in her sleep, dreaming of black collars turning white every time he shook his head.

Revenge grew from a little daydream in the corner of her mind to the 3-D vehemence of cinematic vengeance, an OCD capable of afflicting up to ten scorned women at a time. Calling him while lying under another man, a lover taken for not being him. Slicing up Sam into tiny curls of sub-Sams with a blunt butter knife. Acting hormonally haywire and high-strung in a public place where jazz and blues played seven nights a week. Flinging pasta on pristine walls, his personal fishwife.

Each scenario starting with him whole and ending with him broken into a hundred little pieces and pleading for mercy, for a drop of water, for her. He had to compensate for the mess he left inside her, plagiarise her pain. Being put on silent mode was too taxing, too toxic. Even the roses were looking down on her! She put them into a plastic bag and threw them in the garbage chute and the room was haunted no more by a perfume past.

That night she slept deeply. Gabbar still tied Sam to a pole in her dreams but she refused to budge despite being a renowned dancer with two right feet. She was now she-devil.

The structure and shape of Sam's comeuppance consumed her waking hours. The means were overwhelming to plot, with her mind refusing to see beyond the end. The damage had been deep inside her and deep inside him was where she hoped to wreak havoc.

It was at night that a personal advice column in a magazine caught her eye. 'What should I do?' a girl asked, after having slept with a relative. The answer pointed to various products in the market billed 'morning-after' pills. *OhMyGod*, thought Mira, *I never even wondered once if that would happen to me – pregnancy!* Then she regretted not having conceived, her mind temporarily drifting from mission at hand. Regret, regret all night so that she woke up biting her nails in the morning.

'But I could well have been,' she thought and settled for the maternity route. He had used no protection and this was a time-tested traditional ploy to scare the shit out of hit-and-run men. He had hit her below the belt, so would she. 'Make an honest woman of me,' she'd say most dishonestly.

But he could be certifiably sterile! She'd look a proper slut then, like if this isn't yours, then it must be…er…whose? The option of pulling out the cushion – *ta-da!* – was always there but it had a circus-clown ring to it. *Not your baby, oops, not a baby at all!* Look, she told herself sternly, just get off your ass. Meet him, tell him off. If there was some way he'd know he couldn't be the dad, she'd fall on his head and pull out every hair in plan B. The main thing was making him meet her eye.

Hello, she was going to say, *remember me, remember when we met? Seems I was ovulating then.* And they would sip tea and talk about his paintings and her missing periods. So civilised. How nice when he proposed because she was going to be mommy and he daddy and they could be mommy-daddy together, take their relationship to the next level.

Since it was now six months, the baby would have to be visible in her belly and this called for a minor addition to her person, namely a padding. With a little apology to her uterus, Mira strapped on her latest accessory, the sweetest little bonny cushion you ever saw. The way to a man's heart, her mother used to say, was through his stomach. Mira exulted at having found a new route, through *her* stomach.

She applied for leave and was frozen with fear the entire fortnight it took for the leave to be approved. In the end it was a matter of someone suppressing a yawn long enough to read the application and then fumbling for a pen to sign on the dotted line. She mumbled sad mouthfuls about her mother, sister and father, and swiveling from one pseudo-sympathetic colleague to another, managed to extricate herself for a month.

Mr Shetty called her into his room on her last day of work. 'Just relax. Everything will be all right. Fresh air, lots of fresh air,' he said, adding playfully, 'Promise me.'

'OK,' agreed Mira, who found him no more or no less peculiar than usual.

Her landlady alone was distressed. 'How long will you be gone?' she asked brokenly. Mira was the only one she knew who was as interested in her husband as she. Now she'd have to store all the details till Mira returned, what if she forgot something crucial?

She clutched her husband's elbow emotionally, but as they watched Mira walk out of the gate, her backside in a bit of a bobble, he could barely keep his breakfast down.

~

9

While the family waited for Mr Lalan's head to bob up from *The Times of India*, a ribbon of cool breeze curled in from the window which was shattered an hour ago by some cricket-playing brats on the street. Sam could see shards still glistening under the ledge where a grumpy maid had wielded the broom. The sphere-shaped hole in the glass was surrounded by cracks of different lengths looking like an artist's version of the sun. To Sam, the fact that the sun was yet to set added some poignancy to this imagery.

Mr Lalan emerged from the headlines in time to catch the asinine look on his son-in-law's face. 'So, Samundar, you have decided to quit your job?' he asked, summing up what his wife and daughter had been telling him the whole week in high pitch and low pitch, sometimes in the same sentence.

'Yes, papa.'

'And you do not want to wait till you have secured a better post elsewhere?'

'No, papa.'

The newspapers rustled violently, but Mr Lalan's voice remained reasonable when he asked Sam if he had any idea of his future plans. Only he called Sam Samundar, which was in some contrast to Sam calling him papa instead of the usual nothing.

'I want to paint, papa,' Sam announced with a touch of defiance, thinking of the many times the older man had gone on about oceanic motions and plate tectonics and their intimate connect with each other while Sam had sat there smiling and nodding.

'Houses?' sneered Mr Lalan. 'You will whitewash houses?'

'You misunderstand. I am not talking about whitewash though I don't think there's anything wrong with that...'

'Papa, Donx wants to be an artist. *Artist!*' Delta intervened to avoid a detour into macho trivialities. At this juncture she remembered how Sam had kissed her that first time. Not because it was a nostalgic moment per se but because he now wore the same expression. She had turned to him in this very same room to ask him if he was game for a movie at Regal when he had kissed her with such militancy that she had presumed a long suppressed passion on his part. This flattered her into emergency longings on her own part and before long they were exchanging greeting cards, the mandatory step to marriage in Gujarati communities.

'I have already bought canvas and oil paints,' added Sam proudly.

Mr Lalan cleared his throat. His wife and daughter turned to him hopefully. 'Can't...all this be done side by side, you know, with a job?' he asked.

'I will be forty in three years. I want to start when I am still young. I don't want to be one of those people who are so bitter in their old age for having ignored their real calling in life...Oh, I don't mean you, papa. You have kept up your interest in geology in the most enviable manner. In fact, that is what inspired me,' finished Sam weakly.

Mr Lalan ignored the reference to himself. His face impassive, he was thinking, *Look at him lying to himself, the accomplished liar!* The intellectual dishonesty of the mildly educated secretly appalled him. There was no passion in their academic pursuits, merely a middleclass need to bolster CVs.

Some day, Sam was thinking, this man will come to me pleading that I and I alone do his portrait. And I will agree on the condition that he pose nude, wearing only his habitual expression – that of someone in the process of passing stones. Which, if it happened, would be a landmark feat of self-geologising. The incongruity of this kept Sam pleasantly occupied.

'I think, Samundar,' said the family patriarch gravely, 'you need to think seriously before you go putting in your papers. Once the tag of insanity sticks, it sticks.'

'I have already quit, papa,' said Sam not without some triumph.

If Leela-ben initially worried that her son's inane desire to quit his job would be aided and abetted by his self-consciously unconventional wife, she now gnawed her lip for a different reason. Her widowhood had left her with mixed feelings about her late husband. Immediately after the funeral, which had been strange enough with her eldest sister-in-law howling the loudest and rekindling gossip about a possible romance between them before Mr Shah married Leela-ben, she had been inundated with a sense of relief. By the time his first death anniversary rolled by, she was almost lightheaded with joy. To have hated a man she lived with in a dull, futile way for fourteen years had been a secret she had kept even from herself. He had drained her in every way, that...man.

Mr Shah, whose family ran a successful soap factory courtesy a heavy hand with carbolic, had done nothing but spend money left, right and centre until a truck crashed into his car when Sam had just turned ten. The backseat had been ripped out with Mr Shah still in it and though the newspapers ran only black and white pictures of the accident, Leela-ben could still make out the lack of surprise on his face. He had passed from life to death the way he had lived his whole life, in a stupor.

Leela-ben rejoiced in the sudden freedom that ensued. When he was alive, her husband had made it difficult for her to focus on what was most important to her – her son. Why, her sister Uma-ben was even now under constant surveillance after her husband retired from his job. Recently she'd said, 'I am not sure what to do with him! He is here 24x7, staring at me. Earlier, I handed him a lunch *dabba* and till six he was out of my hair. I am calling you from the bathroom now so he won't hear me!'

Thank god, Leela-ben thought, for husbands who did not hang around! It was not that Mr Shah had been unfaithful – may be he had been but Leela-ben found she couldn't care less – or uncouth or mean or beat her or drank too much or spat more than necessary except in moments of genuine *paan* crises. It was just that he did nothing! And to Leela-ben, who had all her life done something or the other, this was a fatal flaw in a human being. Even in her pregnancy when the doctors had advised total bed-rest, she had made twelve types of pickles!

At the time, Mr Shah's constant complaints of sore back, toothache, migraine, gas, constipation, loose motions, ingrown toenail,

71

too-fast-beating heart, too-slow-beating heart, throbbing joints etc had shut Leela-ben up forever on the subject of ailments. She had known that would only escalate his own quota of pain and the idea of competing with him did not tempt her at all.

Now with Sam proclaiming in a wild frenzy his decision to paint the sunset, the jacaranda flowers, the clouds, Chowpatty beach, the bhelpuri-waala, bougainvillea and even her Bata chappals, Leela-ben grew fearful of the triumph of nature over nurture. May be it was in his genes, this itch to do nothing. Then another thought assailed her – a more pleasing one this time – at least of the two, her son was the creative one really and not that Delta who was whining in the most conservative way like any old wife.

And then, people would compare son to father and laugh and laugh. You can't shut people's mouths, not mid-laugh. Marrying Delta had only been the beginning of a lifetime of ridicule. A non-wife at home and a non-job for a living! And theirs a community known more for its Ambanis than Picassos. In Amdavad, Picasso Patel would have owned a cement factory that made more money than all his paintings put together!

Mrs Shah did not have to wonder long about Mr Lalan's strategy to combat her son's belated puberty. Faking great support for the arts, Mr Lalan cut off his daughter's allowance. With the stoppage of rent from three movie theatres in Jamnagar, Delta lost some of her gypsy insouciance. She saw a lifetime ahead of eating *paav-bhaaji* off pavement carts, and rushed to beg and plead first with her husband and then with her father – but to no avail. Deep into the night she sat with her mother and in the morning the two bleary-eyed women came out with their chins up.

'You will have to change your ways. There is a baby on the way,' Mrs Lalan proclaimed.

The statement almost caused Mr Lalan to collapse on Hillary Clinton's chest in the newspaper's international page. Having heard of many status-conscious men suffering strokes during leisure time, Mrs Lalan hurried to him. 'You are pregnant?' he asked faintly.

'Not me,' she scoffed. 'Your daughter.'

He waved at her to step back. *Why can't the woman bathe before falling into my face?* 'Delta is...?'

Mrs Lalan nodded. 'You can't let the kids starve now,' she said and did not take a shower the whole day.

Mr Lalan had no choice but to obey the womenfolk and loosen purse-strings. To counter the tragedy of being bankrupted by own kith and kin, he turned passionately and simultaneously to geomorphology, sedimentology and paleoclimatology.

10

Hanging out in Stuti's house was a treat for Delta. It was so nicely higgledy-piggledy you didn't have to worry where to place the glass or cup as the wet rings left behind went well with the unwashed curtains, threadbare cushion covers and a carpet that hadn't had the dust beaten out of it since birth.

Her own dwellings demanded constant change. Delta needed to be surprised and immediate environs were no exception. When she suggested alterations in other people's homes, not the least because they paid her ridiculous fee, she had to keep available upholstery, geometric parameters and the matter of their own taste in mind. When it came to the interiors of her own house – incidentally, a donation from dad – she could just charge about on her invisible horse and bring down any wall she wanted with the most grotesque of colours. Sam did not mind what she did to their interiors as long as the stairway, the plumbing, carpentry or the walls were not his department, and their flat was neither the best nor the worst in the neighbourhood.

This, Stuti's place, was a sty, a happy, smelly, roly-poly unashamedly sty-styled sty. Entire walls were made up of old books and one sneezed from the dust at regular intervals. Stuti had halfheartedly graduated in English Literature along with Delta and hung on to every book she ever met.

After a life-saving pee – it did not matter that peeing was the last thing she did before leaving home, it was always the first thing she did upon arrival anywhere – Delta announced, 'I am not myself.'

Stuti had to agree, Delta *was* a mobile ad for multiple brands. With catalogues splaying their stuff on the internet, the entire planet was her flea market. 'All the world's a supermarket aisle, and all the men and women merely shoppers,' Delta often misquoted the Bard.

Delta sneezed. 'Sam has quit his job and is sitting at home, waiting to be daddy.'

'He'll be thrilled. All men are thrilled to be promoted from husbands to daddies.' Stuti had promoted her husband twice before he left her for another woman.

'I think I am pregnant.'

'Think? How can you *think*? Either you are or you are not.'

Delta said hesitantly, 'I will be sooner or later.'

'Not as easy as everyone thinks. Shyam's been trying with that utterly-butterly bitch for two years now, you know. Mine were accidents, they just happened. Keep trying, that's all I can say.'

Delta blanched at the prospect of indefinite sex with her husband.

'I know, I know, in all the old movies, the flowers brush just once and the heroine starts vomiting but in real life your eggs are never in the mood. Here, have some tea.'

Delta picked up the cup gamely. Stuti's brews were only a touch superior to her own, which were undrinkable to begin with. Sam was always picking on her inability to serve tea the *right* way. Her way being to wait till the guest had almost reached the front door and to say very doubtfully, 'Would you like some tea then?' Who, Sam wailed at her, in their right mind would say yes to that? Of course, occasionally, somebody *would*, and then Delta would go into shock and Sam would be wrong and all three of them, including the guest, would form a brief tableau before one of them retracted. The *right* way, according to Sam's mom, was to run into the kitchen and bang pots noisily, swearing, 'You will not leave without tea', even if the guest is saying earnestly that doctors have told him tea can be fatal for him.

Stuti's tea was as vile as Delta imagined it would be. The smell of un-scrubbed saucepan mixed with stale milk and no cardamom to soften the blow when sugar met the tongue.

'So?' prompted Delta, to which Stuti fell instant prey, prattling on about her belly-dancing class and pole-dancing class and how in all these places she met only creepy pot-bellied men who used the F word in a personal context.

'Surprise, surprise,' said Delta dryly.

'Don't be so...It is because you have Sam.'

'Yes, I have Sam,' Delta sighed. A little into the marriage, she had met a man here, a man there, with enough zip to suggest fast and furious detours. But no, she had shaken her head, because she wasn't like *that*. She wasn't like *that* for a long while, she was moral and faithful and Sam-ful for two whole summers. And then it came, an inside job, so to speak. Then, and only then, did she go out and pop her extra-marital cherry. What to do, she just didn't have the inner resources to keep herself entertained like Sati-Savitris obviously did. God knows, she had held on to her legs as long as she could.

A giggle escaped her as she remembered the boys who came on to her in the past. At the time she had gasped, rolled eyes, made jokes or moral little speeches and once even slapped hard. Men are after only one thing and all that. As a schoolgirl, she had believed you only had to kiss a boy to get pregnant. Her mother had, in her maternal quest for purity in offspring, kept Delta from the baser facts of life, as she thought of them, as long as she could. So testicles were tiny spectacles to test your eyes with, blue films were small-budget documentaries shot in shades of blue. And when a boy in her class said he wanted to kiss her, Delta had sternly informed God, 'I am not ready for babies!' The boy got bolder, sent her I-love-you cards with explicit hearts in them to her home address so that she had to confront him one recess.

'Listen,' she said urgently to him, 'don't send me cards, my parents will...'

But he had looked back at her with such bovine lovesickness that she had at once understood the futility of her cautioning and resigned herself to his relentless romancing. For her birthday, he recorded fifteen Hindi film songs on love as a gift for her. Delta gave the tape to her maid, who constantly played it in her room so that Delta had no choice but to hear clunky declarations of love involving hair, lip, eyes, moon, stars etc and picture this boy mouthing all of it. He continued to scribble on walls and in lifts that he loved her and only her. It was disconcerting to find her first name coupled with his surname in flagrant graffiti on school walls – Delta Bhatt.

Unable to fight his sustained devotion any longer, she had cornered him during a school picnic in Elephanta caves and allowed with suitable submission, 'Okay, you can kiss me', and he had kissed her passionately…on the cheek! Then he had stared at her with his signature idiocy as if he had indeed impregnated her.

Even meeting Sam, her second romantic fit, did not clear Delta's head on matters of the heart. There was such *detail* to attend to when it came to setting up home and the posturing against marital domesticity and staidness and settling down that Delta found love the one thing perfectly circumventable. She knew that a man's love, unlike parental love, was no sure thing. It was not as simple as a blowjob in the car while driving down a deserted lane or a khichdi cooked bland when he had the sniffles.

'Women must date like men,' she advised Stuti, leaning back. 'Have different men for different things.'

'I guess so,' shrugged Stuti, still peeved at her own lack of partner.

'One to take you to the dentist.'

'Hot sex,' Stuti hooted. 'One for hot sex.'

'One who fixes you breakfast in bed and won't forget your birthday.'

'One to listen to all your cribbing on the phone.'

'One who makes you laugh so hard you need a diaper.'

'And one to be the daddy of your child,' added Stuti.

'Yeah,' agreed Delta listlessly. And not just any child. Sam's child. It had all begun with Sam. And so it must all end with Sam. She was, after all, Sam's wife.

'Wife!' thought Delta, and was immediately swamped by the word. Perplexed and at a complete loss. Wife was eternal, generic, segregated, like a species with its own scientific name and theme song. In the initial days when Sam introduced her to colleagues, acquaintances, anyone as his 'wife', she actually saw the word disfigure itself in air like a cinemascope special effect until some other verbal deformity diverted her attention.

'Sam is me,' she often told her mother, because after so many years of marriage that was true. Sam was her and she was Sam, they were one but then she'd wanted...company. On her way out of Stuti's place, Delta paused in the lift, waiting for the other passenger – a man with a laptop slung across him – to get out first. Just as she thought, butt-gorgeous!

Next morning, Sam's study of the sky – were the clouds really made of smoke rings? – was interrupted by Delta slowly sliding down the banister, shouting 'whee'. More than her leisurely descent into the living room where he stood, he was mildly distracted by the matter of her nudity. In the early days of their courtship, she had always managed to unsettle him by showing a little nipple here or thigh there in public when no one was looking. By and by, he had trained himself to not take her flashing personally.

He stole a look at her breasts – perky or sulky? – as a purely male reflex when confronted with uncovered breasts. But he told his hands, 'Quick, go hide', and began to draw arabesques in the air in a way he imagined seasoned artists did. Idle fingers were Delta's playthings.

Halfway down she replaced the whee with 'I am acting so strange, na?'

'No, I am the one acting all strange. Wanting to paint in my middle age etc,' he insisted in all humility.

'No, no, *I* am strange. I mean, look at me, Donx,' she invited. Then she squealed, cupping herself between her legs as something sharp met her at the end of the banister.

'Have you hurt yourself?'

'No,' she brushed him off. 'Did you notice I've cut my hair shorter'.

He smiled fondly. How on earth could anyone cut their hair *longer*?

After a pause, she again turned to him with a determinedly zany smile. 'Remember the first time you kissed me?'

'You mean the first time we kissed or the first time *I* kissed *you*?' Having had to take the lead in matters intimate from time immemorial with her, Sam always made it a point to record levels of participation.

'What's the difference?' she asked, losing some of the zany.

'The first time we kissed, you kissed me,' he pointed out triumphantly.

'Wait a minute,' said Delta, forgetting about seduction for the moment. 'Let's get this straight. Remember when we were sitting in my house?'

'I remembered it recently...'

'It was I who remembered it recently, not you,' Delta corrected him imperiously. 'In the same room I had asked you if you wanted to go for a movie...'

'You asked me if I was gay. And anyone knows that is a come-on.'

'Why would I ask you if you were gay? The whole colony knows you pawed Lakshmi Reddy while playing basketball during your South Indian phase.'

'I did not! She just kind of flopped down on my elbow and I was only extricating my hand from under her skirt. If she got turned on, it's sad,' he said indignantly, adding, 'And let's not forget you asked me if I was gay knowing full well I wasn't just to get me to do something to you.'

'I must have been asking if you were *game* for a movie – game! – or something and you just pounced on me when I was halfway through the word. As if I'd ask you such a thing anyway. I'd know if you are or not!'

And now that Sam knew her well, he had to agree that she wasn't the type to ask him anything of the sort if she thought anything of the sort. She drank tea in little glasses from roadside stalls, kept their bedroom windows curtain-less, loved Rajasthani thalis, got her haircuts at barbershops and wore a white sari the day Michael Jackson died. She took considerable pains to be broadminded.

They both stared at each other. The full realisation of the quicksand quality of the foundation of their marriage began to sink in. 'Now is not the time,' concluded poor Delta, 'to spring a fake pregnancy on my husband.'

Mira suffered no such qualms. Having discovered that Sam had got a transfer back to Mumbai only to resign, she booked herself on a flight to that city. In a corner of the departure lounge, she yanked the cushion out from under her tent-like dress minutes before her Mumbai flight was announced and sighed with relief at being able to scratch the skin gone itchy beneath. No one noticed except a woman who had miscarried two months ago and had been enviously watching the bump, thinking there must be little feet and little thumb in little mouth.

Mira tightened her seatbelt and watched an airhostess mime the safety rules. For the first time in her life, she did not care if the flight crashed. If she did not meet Sam in this lifetime, she would in the next – she was sure of that. In a newfound gesture of solidarity with her single status, Mira held hands with herself: that is, she put her left hand into her right hand and clasped tightly. Then she crossed legs, trapping one leg under the other so that she played footsie with herself. This, however, brought her feet into direct view. 'A pedicure!' they gasped on their deathbed. ASAP, Mira consoled glibly.

As the cab nosed into the traffic, she craned her neck to catch a glimpse of her ex-beloved's city. She directed the cabbie from Santa Cruz to Anysmallhotel in Andheri, which was where he resided in the official records. It wouldn't do to arrive at his doorstep without the bump. At the Sadabahar Hotel, Mira hesitated. Garish film posters were stuck outside with blouses torn off the heroines, their chests covered with Marathi graffiti instead. Inside her room a light bulb spat and hissed when she switched it on, and cockroaches scuttled for cover. Off-white blobs in the basin that wouldn't wash away, the crack at the bottom of her teacup and she felt at the end of her tether. But a collapse into sleep and a sluggish awakening restored her resolve and everything came back to her: vendetta on a shoestring budget.

She rubbed the sleep from her eyes. What was that again, yes, reclaim all the runny parts of her. 'Let's find out what's on the other side of the break,' she chirped to the bathroom mirror, fluffed the cushion and reinserted prop for the performance of a lifetime.

~

11

No one knows why Samundar Shah kept his stomach empty that day. He had long gotten used to rummaging for cereal in the mornings as the kitchen fires were kindled only noon onwards when the cook could fit them into her busy schedule. But that fateful morning, the morning of his double-daddy day, he was running short not only of breath but also on carbs. There were three large gins from last night sloshing around at the bottom of his small or long intestines, he wasn't sure which, along with canned orange juice.

The day had begun perfectly normal, if foodless. He was sitting there when Delta finally decided to inaugurate the day and had sashayed nudely down the banister at half past eleven. They had discussed their first kiss and then she calmly buttered some bread slices with suspicious green spots on them, hummed 'Crazy kiya re' without going into a previous or later refrain, gargled with coffee, dropped milk all over the stove, on the sink, on the floor before looking at the clock with a gasp. 'Yashodamma not coming?'

Sam grunted. His wife was essentially a bread-omelet girl and they, by extension, were a bread-omelet couple – the kind of people who'd actually kill the goose that laid the golden egg just because that egg couldn't be fried. Any other type of breakfast, including typical Gujju fare, Delta dismissed as emotional. He went back to the newspapers, hoping to find meaning in black and white. A picture, a graphic, a word, anything can awaken his sleeping giant of a talent. All he had to do was patiently wait for his muse to arrive...

'I said it is twelve and Yashodamma hasn't come,' grumbled his wife.

'The kitchen will stink a day longer, that's all.'

'In my house there were always five servants at any given time,' said Delta, picking up a pair of dhobi-delivered pajamas still on the sofa from a week ago and inserting feet one after the other into them. 'One to cook, one to clean, one to do the gardening, one to drive papa's car and another just to play with me.'

'I am the fifth servant, is that what you are trying to say? I am the one papa hired to play with you?'

'Did I say that? *Did I say that?*'

'What did you say?' he asked sulkily, scanning the headlines.

Delta tied the pajama strings tightly around her waist in a double knot that would need Sam's help or the kitchen knife during a bathroom emergency. 'All I said was my friends are coming for lunch to celebrate and now who'll do the cooking?'

'Your friends are coming here again? They were here just day before!'

'Don't be like that, Donx. In fact, they want to congratulate you.'

'For quitting my job?' he asked, brightening.

Well, thought Delta with deep remorse, there was nothing left to do but lie or die. 'For becoming a father.'

Sam shot up from his chair. 'You mean we managed...? And so soon?'

Delta refused to meet his eyes, mumbling, 'You are so, you know, virile.'

Left to herself, she would not have made this grand announcement, but her dad had told a friend of hers who had called home and one thing led to another and now here she was throwing a party to impending motherhood, only less impending than everyone thought. But what was this, Sam was picking her up tenderly.

'You are carrying my child, you are carrying little Donx,' he murmured and swept her dangly pajama strings aside to see her stomach better. 'I salute you,' he said between kisses on her stomach, 'I salute your womb, I salute your womanhood, I salute Mother India…'

'OK, OK,' she said hurriedly, worried that Yashodamma may walk in and think them engaged in some weird form of oral sex.

Walking out of the hotel, Mira hailed a cab. More and more she was starting to feel unreal. It was all right to lie in her own familiar bed and plot mayhem, but to be out and about in an unfamiliar place and keep her wits around was a huge challenge.

Let me start at the beginning, she would think and then backtrack to the moment when he said he had to leave. On that fateful night he had removed his clothes, then her clothes as she had been too paralysed. There had been an abrupt tremor, an urge to just loll about with him and chat her heart out. To discuss the boys who almost got her, the boys who had paid her a compliment or said things to her she only later in hindsight realised were passionate intentions, the boys she had missed out on simply because she had no sense of the present tense or the deep isolation her soul was about to plunge into and of course the boy who wrote a letter to her in red ink that she later came to think of as his heart's blood. All those boys had culminated in him, Sam, she had wanted to tell him that.

After he had slept off, she sat quenched, with a form in her lap, filling up columns of did you enjoy your stay, will you come again, how was the food, the hygiene etc, unspeakably happy to be asked her opinion. Oh to go back in time and yawn when he read out the time. 'Yes,' she said belatedly, freaking the cabbie somewhat. 'It is five-thirty, so what? Didn't we just step off the clock?'

The cabbie told her it was not five-thirty yet, that it wouldn't be five-thirty for another five hours, madam.

'Do not piss here,' requested a wall. Huh! Not even if the wall begged on bended knee. She adjusted the cushion on her stomach. She had been the dunce of every man's dreams, fired after fellatio, curtains on opening night. Embarrassing herself with impromptu flashbacks was handy in keeping her on track. If she did not inject a little venom now and then into her veins, she might find herself ridiculous and that ridicule may become an antonym to the hate and she may reverse-pedal the vicious cycle and end up back at the aching and the hankering and the beauteous beginnings of them. Before tear no. four thousand, three hundred and sixty-one – the very last tear – rolled down her cheek. Before the spread-eagled legs and the sweet nothings and that first primal scream of a stare.

To slay her dragon she invoked all her childhood heroes – Jhansi ki rani, Chacha Choudhari, Mandrake, Phantom, Hanuman and gadadhari Bheem. She was all of them against a single solitary Sam. A clap of thunder made her start. *Let that be the first drummer of my summer rain.* Lightning rippled white against the sky. 'Shake loose a shower for me,' she coaxed the clouds. She had to repossess herself before somebody else did again.

By the time their guests dropped in, Sam was locomotive with joy. He pulled Stuti into his arms for an impromptu jig, poured fruit juice into their best glasses, causing some breakage and rendering the glass-set an odd number under his wife's mathematical eye, and collected the pizzas with a bhangra whoop that the deliveryman had to accept in lieu of a tip.

'I am going to put up a website in the baby's name,' declared Sam, sprawled in his favorite wicker armchair. 'Click and you can see him everyday.'

'Him?' asked Stuti.

'Him. Her. Doesn't matter.'

'Of course, it does. If there's any justice in the world, men will have only daughters. That's the closest they'll come to knowing our pain!'

'Not again,' groaned someone. Delta's friends were comfortably comatose in Delta's home. The gigantic 'Sexy Mama' card they brought lurched against a wall and they themselves lolled somnolent among the maverick mul curtains and copper-zari cushions. The pale white walls amplified every movement, accentuated the slightest colour, while a driftwood apparition with long, arching hands that looked now meaningful, now meaningless – depending on your mood – haunted the centre of the room.

'We've seen too many baby albums and birthday videos not to thirst for blood. I am going to be obnoxious about our kid's first word, first step. In fact, you can't get me to shut up,' Sam crowed.

'I hate newborn dads,' said one friend, and Sam, his vision blurred by her halter-neck top, felt a sudden urge to take her from behind, doggie-style. Such Stone-Age attacks were a legacy of his time with Mira. She had no business planting her hips so firmly in his mind, turning him into this ass-oholic. Quickly he launched into Bollywood trivia, to which Delta spewed her rehearsed repartee, having perfected it over hours of TV-induced trances.

The five friends swiveled their five heads obligingly but sided with Delta. Sam lapped up their snobbery in unspoken acceptance of his inferiority – financial, educational and sartorial. Her social circle was part of her dowry, what she brought into the marriage. Marrying up was a form of evolution, he had once told his mother, it was a social-climbing of the soul.

'You will lose your figure,' said someone, returning to the topic of the day not without some malice. 'You will become fat post-baby.'

'More of her to love!' Sam said indulgently.

'Yes, daddy,' the five screamed.

'And now,' said Sam, 'I shall go bathe.' They had been calling him daddy ever since they came and he felt impassioned enough to seek some privacy. Moments later he returned happily spent only to find every inch of pizza gobbled up and gone.

'Shall we order some more?' Delta asked with her usual vagueness.

'No, I'm cool,' he said. It would take ages for the man to return even if the ads said half an hour. Not that their fridge would yield anything edible, still he opened it optimistically: sun-dried cherry tomatoes, tofu in much profusion, five bundles of leeks, moldering gooseberry preserve, past-life mushrooms, three barking-empty ice-cream cartons and the faint whiff of corpses. Between Yashodamma and Delta, if he got his ice cubes in summer, Sam considered it divine intervention.

Actually, now that he thought about it, he did not feel very hungry, the contents of his refrigerator vaguely nauseating him. After bidding a touching farewell to every last friend of hers, he turned around to lingeringly hug his wife. His hand trembled as it returned to caress her over the area he imagined his baby bobbing about. 'Boy or girl?' he asked dreamily. 'We can always go to my radiologist aunty to find out.'

'I'll go get some Maggi from the market for you,' cut in Delta briskly.

He tweaked her nose. 'Wife first, mother later, eh?'

She did not reply.

~

12

'What do you mean he doesn't live here?' Mira was saying to Mr Lalan.

After alighting from the taxi somewhere in the vicinity of Sam's address, lunching at a bistro-like place and reading the newspaper at length, she had at last worked up the nerve to commence with the last leg of her journey. A meandering chat followed with a uniformed guard who stood before the imposing walls of the dove-gray villa, her destination. 'Sam...Samundar Shah,' she'd said when her own name naturally cut no ice with the guard.

'Sam sa'ab?' he said with suitable reverence and escorted her to the front-door which stood half-open in an uninviting way. She had stepped inside gingerly, sat down on the nearest sofa with one hand sternly on her stomach in case the cushion decided to misbehave, and waited, tremblingly, for Sam. She hadn't trembled long when this old man came and told her this was not where Sam lived.

'Not any more,' added Mr Lalan.

Mira looked around. There was a framed photograph of Sam with a boy – his brother perhaps – on the carved rosewood bookshelf in which he looked years younger than the time she met him.

'My daughter,' declared Mrs Lalan, joining her husband. She sat down opposite Mira, clanking the several silver keys hanging down her hip. She stroked them now and then as if to chastise them.

Ah, a sister, thought Mira, looking at the photograph again but unable to take in anybody but Sam. She removed a sequined cushion from the small of her back and put it in her lap. 'But this is the address he put in the office records.'

'That's because they used to live here at that time,' interjected Mrs Lalan, having ordered tea with a rapid eye movement at the maid. 'Very old, na, that record,' she added winsomely. It was rarely that Mrs Lalan felt the need to serve tea and charm at the same venue but there was something vaguely menacing about this girl. Though she carried no luggage, she had the look of a squatter.

With some effort, Mira peeled her eyes off the photograph and fixed them on Mrs Lalan. 'They moved out together?' she asked leaning forward, which caused the unofficial cushion inside her clothes to collide with the official one in her lap.

'Ten years now, isn't it?' Mrs Lalan looked at her husband as if for confirmation, but more to involve him in general chitchat. He was prone to nap in company.

'Delta was just a child then,' Mr Lalan yawned and remembered buying the duplex flat for them so they could end the brief stopover at Sam's mother's home after they left here.

Mira's bewildered 'Delta?' was lost in a burst of barks from an inner room.

'Dachshunds are moody people,' Mr Lalan said, getting up laboriously to go to his dogs.

'Yes,' agreed his wife, her eyes widening of their own accord. 'They never barked to show us you are coming. Now they are impatient to come and say hello to you.'

Mira, who misunderstood her hostess's eye-saucering for awe at canine cavorts, widened her own eyes in polite response, at which Mrs Lalan appeared a little miffed until, a few seconds after Mr Lalan's departure, tea was served.

Mrs Lalan was unnerved to see the girl clutch her stomach even while sipping tea. Overeating of free plane food, tut-tutted Mrs Lalan, having noted the airline tag on Mira's handbag. Aloud she trilled, 'While waiting for Sam, would you like to watch the wedding video? I watch it once everyday.'

This time Mira looked at the photograph properly, her teeth chattering and her toes ten ice cubes. And as she felt herself turning into a vanilla ice-cream family-pack she knew she had exactly one minute to cry. (She couldn't cry buckets because she had no handkerchief and availability of tissues was subject to her hostess's whim.) A truncated montage ran through her head, of him approaching, smiling into her eyes, sweeping the hair off her face, spilling into her. A trumpet blared and across the carpet came a solemn parade of women holding the scarlet letter 'A' to their chest, home-breakers whiplashed and stoned on conservative terrains, witches burnt at stakes, adulteresses all. None made eye contact with her.

Mira started to wane. She was not a woman anymore, but the other woman. *The Other Woman*. Temporarily a chemically preserved mummy at the bottom of a pyramid. 'Children?' she managed to ask through the burst of bile in her mouth. 'Do they have children?'

'Not yet,' said Mrs Lalan demurely.

Mira thought double quick – the man was married. *Quarry husband, quarry husband*, she beeped to her brain, which forwarded the message back to her at the same speed. She still had the option of tucking tail between legs and vanishing without a song and dance about nonexistent offspring. But as she sipped elaichi tea, she slowly regained her poise. If he had wanted her silence, he should've made nice. Or pulled out her tongue. What did bimbettes and coquettes worry about consequence?

Sam reclined on the armchair and gathered his thoughts while Delta gathered pasta. This baby was making him emotional, but what the hell, it was not everyday that he became a dad. *I have to change*, he thought grandly. *I have to grow, to mature. I am not a kid anymore. I am going to have a kid. I will love my wife. At least I will be more polite in my thoughts to her...*

Such were his circuitous thoughts when the telephone rang.

'There is a lady from your office here,' said Mrs Lalan coldly. 'She wants to speak to you.'

'Mommy, don't give the phone. Could be insurance pests...'

'Here she is,' continued Mrs Lalan as if he hadn't spoken.

'Sam? I have been so worried,' began Mira. And that was no lie. She was worried. She had been worried and she was going to worry for a long time to come with the previous worries now replaced by fresh ones.

'Why are you here?' asked Sam when saliva eventually trickled back into his mouth and returned to him the gift of speech.

'You know why,' was the inexorable answer. 'I am expecting!'

'Expecting what?' asked Sam, perplexed by her failure to complete the sentence.

Mr Lalan came on the line then, asking Sam to come over immediately to deal with 'this woman, Mir, who is pregnant with your child'.

'Oh,' said Sam, 'expecting!' Then he heard himself. Crash-bang went the receiver. For long moments he stood there, wondering what to do with the rabbit that he had pulled out of his magician's hat.

'Hello, I am back.'

Sam straightened. Coming up was one loving, loyal wife who was herself in the process of multiplying and therefore not to be exposed to such monstrous gossip that was sure to rush her howling to a barber. Stress always turned her against her hair. He'd go to Andheri, drive Mira to an abortion clinic and that would be that, the nightmare would full stop. He would impress upon the Lalans the total necessity of keeping this from Delta as she was in such a delicate state.

'I have to go out,' he blurted. 'You know that job I applied for.'

She, who never kept track of his words or sentences wedding reception onwards, nodded absently and placed the instant noodle packets and eggs on the kitchen counter. Waaah, she wailed mentally, there goes my cabaret. She'd planned to cook Maggi and curl it here and there strategically on her body – after it had cooled of course – so Sam could eat and then ejaculate. Their future baby needed all the help it could get.

'The guys just called when you were out. I am to meet them right now. In fact, I am late…' Babbling, he ran up the stairs and was down in record time with his wallet snug in his back pocket. He had no idea what off-the-rack abortions cost these days but he couldn't let *her* pay to get rid of *his* baby!

Delta looked at his summer shorts and the hip but home-wear vest she had fabric-dyed with her own two hands. 'Donx darling, it looks like rain,' she began, but he cut her off.

'Casual is in these days, don't you know?' he threw over his shoulder. 'Don't be such a mother-hen.' *Not when I'm being such a father-cock.*

In less than forty minutes, he had exited Ghatkopar and touched Andheri East in a spectacular screech of brakes, I-give-a-damn acceleration, traffic-light hanky-panky and much flashing of the middle finger. He heard thunder; hopefully lightning would spot-strike and render him impotent at the very least. Shit happens, he reassured himself incoherently. Shit. Happens. Shit.

'First things first,' he said, walking into the Lalan living room, having decided to seize the initiative in manly splendor.

'No, first things first,' contradicted Mr Lalan. 'This woman here, this Miss Mir Jacob, is from your Bangalore office. The office which has its head office here that you chose to quit in such a suspicious hurry last week.'

'She is saying you made her pregnant,' wailed Mrs Lalan, breaking into her husband's formal framing of charges.

One look at Mira's burgeoning belly drove out all the smartass sentences Sam had rehearsed along the way. Mesmerised by the bump, he made no further attempt at speech.

He hadn't even known he had a sperm count and now, wow, double whammy! He had heard of so many couple friends who

95

waited and waited before it happened. 'We are trying,' they'd say shamefaced, like weary peasants toiling in fields under an April sun. Most people spoke of 'miracle' babies, hinting at long arduous never-ending attempts to conceive. Why couldn't he shoot blanks like so many other infertile, sterile men all over the world? Why was he alone felled by the Fallopian Tube conspiracy? Maybe he should start a sperm bank – the one-man-stop for global babylessness. *Somebody neuter me, please!*

He was careful all the while to smile a little smile, which he hoped looked more smile and less stool sample, aware that his father-in-law's face was intentionally averted and that his mother-in-law's eyes could dilate any minute. The grapes on the table, unlike him, were seedless. Then his gaze slowly travelled upward, departing from Mira's belly to arrive at her eyeballs. Wide-eyed, under-slept, slipshod, nerve-frayed, she looked back at him in a freeze shot.

Face to face with her assassin, Mira felt her limbs atrophy. All the hellcats in latex banging at her halted their fists – she wouldn't let them in now, they'd have to wait till she got this moment out of her system. Till she forgot his face, his voice, his tongue on her tongue.

Twang went Mira's heart. *Here is the first man to put me on the moon!* It broke her to see the carefulness in his eye, the cautiousness. She was the destitute at his door, the beggar-maid seeking alms, the psycho Cinderella come to find her slipper. Nothing was real. Nothing was magical. Like the flowers in the vase on the Lalan TV. Synthetic and scentless and surreal. Mira feared she would faint or do something that felt natural only for now – like stand up to sing the national anthem. Head spinning, off-kilter, like an empty teapot tilted to a brimming cup, her brain was going non-linear on her.

'Miss Mir, tell me, have you met this man before?' asked Mr Lalan.

'Mira,' corrected Sam absently, involuntarily answering the question. 'She is M-i-r-a.'

'Myrrh,' counter-corrected Mira, who thought her one lie so singularly gruesome that she industriously wanted to maintain all other honesties by him. 'I was baptised Myrrh. But no one we knew knew how to say it. They said 'Myrrh-*aa*?' and at that time my sister who was little started calling me Mira. In my degree certificate, passport etc I'm Myrrh Celestine Jacob. Neither here nor there, of course. The thing is my name is Myrrh. M. Y. R. R. H.'

For a long minute the Lalans and Sam stared at her equally pole-axed. Mira looked back defensively. She wasn't going to apologise for her parents' poetic bout at the sight of their firstborn. They must have named her thus to rhyme with – what? The fan's whirr. The tiger's grrr... 'Myrrh!' she called herself to attention.

Sam shook his prematurely graying head. 'In a nutshell...'

She nodded receptively, a squirrel at his picnic.

'...I mean, why did you come *here*?'

Mr Lalan spluttered, 'This is the address you wrote down in your records, you pauper, as you had no house of your own when you married my daughter. I got you the job, I got you the house, now...' The idiot incarnate!

'Puppa!' called out Mrs Lalan, who had zeroed in on this form of name-calling when in a drunken fit following Delta's birth Mr Lalan refused to accept paternity. Which was also the real reason why their daughter was named so pet-name-ishly. 'Let's call her Delta then, as three parties were involved in making her,' he had said nastily. To emphasise his paternity and her own fidelity, Mrs Lalan regularly called him Puppa.

'Puppa,' she cried again, but it was Sam who looked at her obediently. If nothing else, fatherhood was definitely his new vocation, he grasped. 'He is going to cut off the money again, don't you see?' pointed out Mrs Lalan to Sam, thinking Sam's laid-back air a little inappropriate. 'It is only because of Delta's good news that he...Now look what you have *done*.'

What he had *done* was fill up a uterus not allotted to him. Sam squeezed his temples hard to bury the migraine in the back of his skull. From the corner of his eye, he spied Mira on the sofa and suddenly felt too tired to stand himself. He wanted to sink his head into a soft, soft lap and go to sleep for a long time only to wake up to a flat-bellied, non-procreating, vasectomised world. He had just wanted to go skinny-dipping, who knew his penis could be so lethal when unsheathed? Why had he made love without all those condoms he had purchased? 'Made love'? Hell, that was what Delta said. He hadn't the faintest what Mira called what they did.

Strengthening his resolve, he turned to Mrs Lalan. 'I will take her to a hospital and get rid of it right now.'

'Nooooooo,' sang Mira from her corner of the sofa. 'I mean I am not giving up this child.'

'Are you sure?' asked Sam politely.

Mira nodded. For this was one thing she was positive about – if she had been pregnant with anyone's child, even Sam's, she would have gone ahead and had the baby. Her parents and Maya had hardly anything to do with her anyway. She could pass off the baby as adopted or a friend's the rare times they all had to socialise, like at Maya's death or something.

'You will have my baby?' enquired Sam because he still couldn't believe it, but Mira squirmed for the first time since she planned this jaunt. She wasn't ashamed that they had once been lovers and that she planned to scratch his eyes out, she wasn't even ashamed of this pretend baby they had made. She was ashamed of a fantasy in which she had run around with him – *this husband of some other woman* – in a garden where birds warbled and violins played. She was ashamed because in all their covert coupling he had never hinted at flora or fauna. Had she hallucinated just that wee bit?

'Yes,' she said in a more subdued way, 'I will.'

'Think about it,' said Mr Lalan, who understood the compulsion to first get rid of extra fittings before dealing with son-in-law's terminal stupidity. He said in the most paternal tone he could summon that a baby out of wedlock was never an easy option. 'Tongues will wag and people will associate the child with shame and dishonour.'

Mira radiated a mutinous aura.

And, Mr Lalan continued, where would she find the money to bring it up?

'It will be just a small baby. How much will it need?'

Mr Lalan marveled at such shortsightedness. This woman and his son-in-law were a match made in heaven! 'Infants are small to begin with, then they are toddlers and then teenagers and adults, so on and so forth. At each stage, even if they don't physically grow and stay midget all their life due to genes or malnutrition, they need many things, including education, entertainment and other care, which will deplete your bank-balance at every step.'

99

Mira saw where he was going with this. 'He will support me,' she said carelessly, pointing at Sam.

'*He?*' Mr Lalan lost his mature deportment. '*He* is jobless. *He* can't support himself.'

'So what do you recommend?' demanded Mira, falling back on her terminology with Mr Shetty as Mr Lalan looked kind of official. Any moment she expected to be tumbled down with 'balance-sheet', 'audit report' and 'non-performing assets'.

'That you don't deliver,' he thundered.

A curious gurgling noise filled the air, which was Sam retching. Mira watched the pearly white liquid fly out of her former paramour's mouth and land on the Lalans' carpet to the extreme left of her sandal. Sam's beautifully sculpted lips that had haunted her own lips on so many nights in so many dreams, had nibbled her neck and voraciously eaten out of her heart now pouted to vomit.

'Who is pregnant?' she thought she heard Mr Lalan mutter. Mira made to get up and felt a moment of confusion when she threw the cushion in her lap back to the sofa: was that her baby? No, no…this was a Lalan cushion, not the cushion she and Sam had made. Mira caught Mrs Lalan's eye. 'It is raining,' she said and both women looked out the window for a second.

Sam's mouth was still working though Mrs Lalan had the foresight to poke him in the back until he now stood a distance away from the pure-silk Persian carpet for which Mr Lalan had paid a hefty customs duty.

Sam was saying between retches, 'I did not eat the whole day. Yashodamma did not come, Delta's friends ate up all the pizza. She never made Maggi for me…'

To which Mr Lalan said, 'Stop blaming everybody else. It is time you became a man!' When Sam blinked, Mr Lalan became more blatant. He brought his face very close to Sam's. 'You have no balls,' he told his son-in-law succinctly.

Why did people say that, debated Mira. As far as she knew — from her one and only experience — balls were soft and delicate, dangling defencelessly. In fact, the most feminine part of a man. So, if she had caught Mr Lalan's drift, the correct thing to say would be that Sam was all balls. Of course, Mira did not say this aloud. Mr Lalan looked mad enough to go get a gun.

Bang.

Bang.

One bullet in each bail. Sam's. And then Sam would really have no balls. He suddenly looked dainty to Mira. So dainty.

'Stopped raining,' announced Mrs Lalan.

13

Glad for the respite after Sam split, Delta ruminated over her guilt pangs. Sam's newly strange behaviour complete with paints and easel, she knew, would not have let him fib to her father. He would appropriate an artist's sensitivity even if the talent was yet to appear. If she had said, for instance, 'Let's pretend to be pregnant, Donx', he would have looked askance and rejected the idea outright. His idea of artistic temperament would demand petty honesties of him. No, her mother had been right, it was best to deceive him along with her dad. Her only recourse lay in seducing him ever so often to spin the lie into truth.

Delta was sure about the body and soul being in deep conference with each other. At some point she was sure her soul would update the body, which would promptly fall fertile and make her a yum mum. When one wanted something so deeply, so-so deeply that it seemed to be already a reality, it was only a matter of time. She had anticipated the future and instead of her body calling the shots, she had. The body's task was thus made easy, it only had to follow orders. Stupid body though, not interrupting the menstrual flow, not listening. Which was reason enough to make Sam's mom crow. However much she lamented her lack of grandchildren, this muteness of her womb, Delta knew, was the old woman's ultimate high-five with Sam.

Delta understood the mechanics of her body. It hated to be told. And marriage was telling it big-time and for a lifetime. This house she stayed in, a gift from her dad, could do with another inhabitant. And after so many years of marriage it seemed a bit...celibate or something to not breed. As if inner mechanisms were not being tuned regularly. She had a horror of needlessly visiting doctors and invoking their medical superiority. Until now, she had been content to wait, to believe that it would happen if it had to happen. But now, after having taken fate into her own hands and turned her own scriptwriter, she deemed it time to break the news to Sam's mother over phone.

In under ten minutes when Sam's mother was sitting at the end of her bed, Delta was not so sure. No amount of coaxing that she wait to congratulate them till Sam returned could stop Mrs Shah from tucking in her pallu and ordering her driver hither.

'Lying down is the best. What did the doctor say?'

'That lying down is the best,' repeated Delta, kicking herself mentally for inviting the woman over. But Mrs Shah had other plans for Delta's feet.

'Keep the feet up on a pillow. Did he say that?'

Delta nodded and Mrs Shah was happy to hear that the doctor was in perfect agreement with her. Or else she'd have dragged Delta to Bharat Kikani's obstetrician nephew who was just back from the US and knew all there was to know about pregnant women.

Delta affected fatigue and leaned back with her eyes closed. Mrs Shah could be blinding – she liked her bling.

Contrary to appearances, Mrs Shah was not above eating crow. The news of her daughter-in-law being with child had tugged her wayward mind in every direction – from berating herself for every uncharitable thought ever directed at Delta and the world, to not having prayed enough to family deity and denying Delta that extra glass of mango juice when Mrs Shah had been reasonably sure she wanted it, to not loving her husband enough, to loving her son too much...She began to rub Delta's feet and mouth free advice.

'Throw away your microwave. Don't heat anything in it. You know what it is, cancer on a plate. And you must lie on your back,' said Leela-ben. 'Employ Yashodamma fulltime so that you do not have anything to do. I will loan you my driver until the baby comes but you will only get out of the house to go to the doctor. Never allow the doctor to do an internal examination, you know that's how Jaishri bhabhi lost her baby. Poke, poke, poke with glove-waala hand that choked the baby...And kick Sam out of your bedroom. No more sex!'

'No more sex?' echoed Delta, knowing that Mrs Shah would guide her son too on this and then all chances of shifting the baby from the virtual world into the real one would be lost. 'Sex is fine, that's what the doctor said,' she asserted.

'Doctor!' snorted Mrs Shah. 'Did the doctor get you pregnant? Is the doctor pregnant? Take everything he says with a pinch of Tata salt. No precaution is too much for this baby. Delta beta, this baby is a gift from god, you have to understand that. So, remember, no sex.'

And all Delta wanted to do at that moment, what she had to do to get this baby off the ground, was have sex and more sex. Actually, truth be told, not just for the baby. As long as she could remember, she had wanted to be a porn star. Even after she heard about the poor pay, the diseases, the working conditions, she sometimes envied them their soreness.

Mrs Shah was thinking, thank god she had that talk with her son. If only she had spoken earlier, her grandchild would've been going to college by now! It was Mr Shah's soul trying to re-enter the family...

The two women sat there in the gathering dusk, occasionally exchanging smiles when they got tired of not looking at each other.

'Your hips...we'll just go with caesarean,' Mrs Shah murmured consolingly.

At least my ass doesn't get wedged in doorways, retorted Delta silently.

Indifference was Delta's weapon of choice. It felt blunt enough to her victims but it was something substantial to hold in hand when it was the back of an old woman's skull you wanted to sock. No fingerprints, see. A yawn or a meaningless smile, nobody can take offence and nuances depend totally on the interpreter.

Growing up, Delta had heard enough disharmonies between her parents to sour her on the idea of eternal togetherness. She remembered lying in bed with equal amounts of comfort and discomfort at most of their seesaw act. Her father would want to suddenly uproot himself and settle down abroad in a place her mother could not pronounce. Or he'd wake up one perfectly sane Sunday and over breakfast announce his plans to renovate his old homestead somewhere at the back of Gujarat's throat.

'You go live anywhere,' Mrs Lalan finally put her foot down. 'Delta and I will live here.' She said that she wanted to grow old and senile in surroundings of her own choosing, that she wanted to bid goodbye to the world from the bit of the world she knew and occupied and which she could barely bring herself to vacate.

Delta knew that people considered her upbringing a bit unorthodox. As a child, the cousins who came to spend navratri holidays with them told her breathlessly in bed that the Lalan stairway was ornate, that the food there was endless and that she herself was a tourist attraction.

She was her parents' pet, she knew. Her father handed her his credit card at the slightest excuse. And her mother was always lapsing into her baby anecdotes. 'You stuffed pearls into your nose at the age of two,' Mrs Lalan had said just last week. 'Pearls,' she had repeated, tapping Delta's nose as if it was an oyster.

'Oddball' came to her originally without too much effort. All she had to do was the little things, like sneak the smaller girls for a fag to the garage, back the car into the iron gate, denting both car and gate amidst much giggling, show them pubic coiffures in risqué magazines and then compare their own unruliness to these by torchlight.

'This Delta!' people would say – tuition teacher, neighbour, gardener, friends' mother – and shake their heads, assigning her further roles, provoking her into shocking them more, to be what they could gape at and compare to. Any inactivity on her part was eyed by her audiences with deep suspicion so that at some point her spirit broke and she would give in and give them what they wanted – some small scandal they could just about handle.

Matters came to a head once or twice, Delta remembered faintly, especially when one of her aunts had towed away her offspring, saying she would never come here again as this house was not fit for children. Why? Because of some minor misdemeanor of Delta's. This was proof that she was not an average girl of her times, that she was *different*, that mischief was manufactured somewhere inside of her. Marriage had dimmed this belief, snatched it and crushed it underfoot.

Sam and she lived with her parents for a while and then moved in with his mother for a short spell. Mrs Shah had immediately dismissed the maid, saying now that Delta beta and she herself were around, housework shouldn't be a problem. And Delta had tried, really tried, to be in charge of the garbage.

Sure, hers was a spick and span soul but the corners of that house had been haunted with bastard little ghosts who poked the dirt right back in even as she swept and mopped and cleaned and dusted. This apparently did not happen to real women, who only had to pass by a place for the place to sparkle, like they just pooped diamonds in it.

Then, one day, just like that, Mrs Shah reinstated her old maid. Which was when Delta understood that the whole thing had been a ploy, probably to make her look bad in front of Sam or to assess her 'real' worth. Her eye had actually filled with tears, she who hadn't known how to cry. Mrs Lalan, her own mother, told her like it is. 'This is to break you down.'

When it was time for them to live separately – curiously enough, a move suggested by Mrs Shah herself after the Lalans were kind enough to buy a flat as belated wedding gift – a woman was procured to live in with them. 'She is from the nearby slums and wants only one day off in the week,' said the senior Mrs Shah.

Delta had had to refuse. She knew such an arrangement would mean espionage, of birth control pills and prophylactics and sanitary napkins and all those wasted babies of the future Shah dynasty. Mrs Shah had smiled grimly at Delta's refusal – warfare between them had begun long ago -- much like she smiled now. Then Yashodamma came and organised Delta's home environs, leaving her to disorganise herself thoroughly.

Delta stretched her feet, her lovely baby feet that she took such good care of. This was not a day to spend indoors. She would have loved to race out in her little red car and meet all the big bad wolves out there. People suffered from sexache same as headache or backache! She had discovered this superpower sometime back, the ability to look at a man, one glance, and hook him to her, to touch him lightly, all above-board, and feel his eyes crystallise on her forever, to whisper wetly in his ear, him the only man in the world and she the only woman, to be taken in all the positions there were, to cut the crap and call each other by their first names, names boring people called them all the time but magical now in a new mouth.

But no, she said.

But yes, yes, *yes*, she said.

If you breathe a word of this to anyone, I will personally come and destroy your hairbrush, she threatened herself. It was a threat that worked usually for the hairbrush was her knight in shining armour when all else failed. 'Plus,' she warned herself for good measure, 'I will smash every human knuckle on earth.'

It was a frequent nightmare of hers – to wake up and find that everyone had lost their fingers.

~

14

The sky had mopped itself up though the same couldn't be said of the roads. Stray vehicles that had come to a standstill in the downpour misled traffic at strategic points, leading to a cacophonous outpouring of road rage.

Trying his best to sit still in his car and not tug the steering wheel off, Sam was in a mood to blame the current fiasco squarely on his spouse. Why wasn't she built along the lines of heroines in films and books who calmly moaned on their backs, why couldn't she stroke his ego into solvent erections? Why? Then she'd have fallen pregnant long ago and no stranger would have come knocking on his door – his father-in-law's door to be goddamn precise – saying, like a seventies' film heroine, *mein aapke bachche ki maa banne waali hoon*. In this day and age only heroines in TV soaps kept buns in their microwaves.

A boy selling magazines was moved by the anguish on Sam's face sticking out of the car window. 'Sa'ab,' he said, thrusting a desi *Playboy* at the car window. Inside the mag, Sam knew, were women who'd try to lure him with body parts that he now had access to in twice the quantity he required. Why did gods do this anyway? Why send a downpour when you asked for dew? Look at the women in those magazines — lax legs, eyes afire, every inch an invite.

Everybody he knew was having it off on the side. With women they met on the Net, in the local to Kurla, their neighbour's guest, their niece's best friend and in one desperate case a post-hysterectomy aunt. ('Women may age,' said the lover of the elderly to Sam sagely, 'but there are no senior-citizen cunts.') Why, even at the old college meet-up, two total losers had hooked up for the night. He knew because the counterfoils — three, the showoffs! — had been left under the bed and the sweeper had brought them to his notice in his capacity as meet organiser.

All around him were writhing bodies from whom he was separated only by a thin self-imposed monastic wall, the have-not from the haves. The very knowledge had been foreplay, that people were involved in no-strings-attached, anonymous, caterwauling, cock-defying, cunt-crunching coitus in hotel beds, on floors, in supermarket aisles, elevators, dim hallways and even broom closets somewhere. And, silly him, he had been content to sleep, perchance to wet-dream!

Currently escorting Mira from the Lalan homestead — for some reason named Janaki Kutir — to wherever she was put up, he hoped to soon return her to sender.

Next to him Mira cleared her throat.

'Hi,' he said, giving her a sideways smile, open to truce.

'Do you mean it?'

'I only…'

'I know. But are you really happy to see me?'

Fortunately, a cow stood in their way and had to be skirted with some effort, during which her question went from passionately voiced to a rhetorical one.

Not giving up on the general theme, she said, 'You forgot me.'

He grunted. Did she know men and their bodies? How it made lunatics of them? Did she know there were parts of him that would never forget parts of her until his body was consigned to flames and his skull spluttered out its contents? Oh, he remembered everything, down to the odor of her navel. Could he explain in three simple sentences his fears over losing his mojo? With only Delta for a playmate and acres and acres of bedtime yawning across the rest of their combined lifetime, he was afraid he'd become permanently half-past six like so many men he knew. Soon sex will be what other people did. Would she get it – how it bothered him, the existence of vaginas? That they were many, many in the world, around him, behind him, ahead of him, to the left and right of him and if his car was under a bridge then directly above him, and that they were just there waiting with nothing to do under saris and jeans and skirts and salwars while he was going plain stark crazy here for the want of one of them. That she had one of them, of what he wanted so ravenously.

But for now these words were only sounds at the bottom of his throat. When he turned to her, their eyes in mid-air collision, she suddenly smiled. Carefree, as if there was no subtext, certainly no fetus, between them. She looked so much like she had the very first time they met that he was able to ask what was uppermost in his mind, 'Why did you not just keep this between us? The baby, I mean. Why tell the world?'

He watched her eyes dim like the Diwali diyas his wife strived to keep alight at their doorstep where windy weather fought her wick by wick. 'I would have if you kept in touch,' she said over-reasonably. 'You chose to stay away.'

She wasn't ba-ba anymore, he found out. In bed, under him, she had been yes sir, yes sir, all bags full. And here she was, a regular harridan out of any nightmare. 'I am bad,' he said grandly, 'at keeping in touch. Ask anyone about me, that's the first thing they will tell you. I am not wired to communicate.'

'I know what you thought, that you can handle everything with your silence,' she spat.

'I am married! Surely you got that by now.'

Mira looked ahead, at the incoming rush of road and tar so restful to the eye. 'You were supposed to return. You were supposed to return to explain why you can't return.'

After that, thankfully, she fell silent. Yes, he admitted to himself, he had rolled over and played dead. But that was how it worked, wasn't it? You met, you mingled, you went your way. Tut, tut, went his tongue in public-school accent, Mira was proving such a foolish investment. Maybe if it had been a much-married, kid-harried, tube-tied woman who whooshed him in and whooshed him out in one breath, things would have been much simpler. Sans the clutter of failed birth control anyway.

As Sam maneuvered his car a little farther, daylight began to fade along with his hopes. He watched a man sip from a coconut and thought how easily his brain could replace the fruit. There seemed to be nothing solid inside his head at this moment, his brain was completely potable.

Sam wanted some privacy for the chat they planned, but she refused to invite him into her room, saying there was nothing left to say, really, if he only wanted to harp on the MTP angle.

'N...no,' Sam stammered, taken aback by this abrupt dismissal, but still slumping into the broken-string sofa in the hotel's lobby where at least ten people dedicated themselves to staring solely at them.

Then as he sat there saying nothing at all, she decided to fidget with one of the broken strings fished out gingerly from the sofa and said in soft, agreeable, almost flirtatious tones that this must have all come as a big surprise to him. 'But you see,' she rushed on, 'it isn't like I'm asking for anything.'

He tried. He really tried to give an account of himself. 'When I met you...it's not that I wanted to escape my responsibilities. I just wanted to reinvent myself,' his voice trailed off. However he was to say it, it sounded bad so Sam did not give her the bare bones of his lust argument, of loving his wife and yet not loving her enough on that particular night, that particular hour or, when it came right down to it for those goddamn precise minutes.

'Did I remind you of anyone?' Mira asked with a spark of interest and Sam wished she bloody had. For such deeper stimulus would pave the way for weightier motivation than fuck for fuck's sake and nothing more. It was fitting though, thought Sam, that finesse eluded him now when he needed it most to extricate himself.

'No,' he said truthfully, 'only of someone new.' To him it had been important that it was not his wife. The rest had been up to chance. He would have balked at touching, caressing some known face, at running his finger down a familiar profile. What set her apart was her utter remoteness from his daily life, her distance from his everyday existence, of the utter impossibility of her appearing, say, in his kitchen to reheat her coffee. Not so impossible anymore, he realised with a start.

'I feel like a drink,' he muttered. 'But we can't,' he said awkwardly. 'I mean, you can't...' Being pregnant and all was what he meant.

He stretched his legs to iron out the kinks in his knees and accidentally bumped her ankle. Bad moment there with apologies, much shifting back on the broken down sofa and clearing of throats. Now they sat more straight, their backs like well-placed ramrods, their palms decorously in their laps and not wandering about out on the off-chance of encountering another palm from another hand from another body.

'So you are having it?' he asked gruffly when they had both collapsed into the previous coma before they briefly came alive with that accidental touch.

She nodded promptly.

'Can you manage?' he asked as a horrible thought shot through his head, further hampering his consciousness – did she think they'd marry and play happy families? He blurted out, 'I was just this stranger you met, Mira. How can you plan your whole life around me, leave your own life behind to come chasing me?'

Sam felt the need to restart his blood circulation as keeping his knee out of her way was giving him pins and needles, but he also had to grope for the magical words that would make her go away, melt back into the midnight moments of history or myth. God, how much of per capita crap was he supposed to take, anyway? He was also aware that he did not have much time on his hands. Delta was tapping her foot at home and would summon him on his mobile, which listed him as Donx under D. But Donx was as Donx does and he was – for the first time since he had embarked upon this misadventure of flesh – mortally frightened of the repercussions, of being demoted to plain old Sam from Donx, of abdicating acres of Donkeydom for what was it again? He had a sudden urge to cry, confess to Delta and leave the mess in her capable hands. To go, uh-oh I have knocked up a woman, how bad is that exactly?

But reality was this woman currently by his side, the way her clothes skimmed her lovely lady lumps, her left hip knobby side up, the tight hold she had on her nostrils, the nape of her neck with its single gray hair, sitting there like a bench with a giant 'wet-cement' board. In time he was sure he'd be able to give a brilliant account of himself, but right now, right now he was a void.

He adopted a fake patient voice. 'OK, supposing we go along with the baby, what would you expect of me?'

Mira sifted swiftly through his features, shrugged and bowed her head on that ridiculous stalk of a neck. But he noticed her eyes, they were back to bright. He would have expected her to be more...stifled. Maternity can turn some women, he had heard, stark raving mad.

'I mean,' his voice gathered volume, 'what would my duties be exactly? You know I can just deny the whole thing. I can say we've never met.'

'Two of our colleagues and the hotel liftman have vouched to testify if it ever came down to it,' she interrupted in a hard, cold icicle of a voice, lying through her teeth but confident of procuring such alibis if necessary. 'I filled that feedback form for you in the room, remember?'

Sam remembered no such thing but panicked at the absence of amiability in her face. Tigers crouched in her eyes now and he had no desire to see them spring for his neck. Her eyes were the looping kind, the kind that'd lasso him to her, swing down a vine to territory unknown. And then, as they continued to gaze at each other with personal agendas, Sam felt the flux in his feet. He knew if he tried to stand or walk now he couldn't. He could only sedately sit and wait for the weakness to pass, for the egg-whisk to die down in his blood.

'What will you have me do?' he asked in exactly the defeated voice he thought Mira sought.

Her eyelashes swish-swished as she looked him up and down, from his feverish face to his achy feet. 'An apology for a start,' she said.

'I am sorry. I mean, you know that already, right? I am sorry I lied to you, I am sorry I got you in this condition, this mess. I'm sorry I'm married. I mean, I am happy I'm married, but sorry that you did not know, that I did not tell you...'

She shook her head as if what he said wasn't what she wanted to hear. 'Are you sorry you met me? That we did what we did, said those things...? Would you have remembered me again ever if I had not come here?'

He nodded an appeasing nod. 'I am a married man, what do you expect? I had to forget.'

'Is that why you quit your job? Because it reminded you of me?'

That's when he decided to launch into words selected for their listenability, for their swallowability, for their impracticality at being traded at the stock market. There had been the path of bluntness and he had already taken that and now he would take this, the sugarcoated one. Yes, he said, yes and yes and yes. He was going to give her every yes in him until he had no more yesses to give. So he gave her precisely the bull he had rejected earlier. Bull was how he had got her going in the beginning and bull was how he would evacuate her...

'I love you, you know,' she interrupted, but her eyes remained detached, like this was what she thought she had to say and get over with. It was a pre-recorded voice, a voice from the past when love had dignified and sanctified their mismatch.

'I...' *Don't say it, don't say it, Sam...*'love you too.' The words fell clunky on the floor, bottom-heavy. Obviously, saying the right thing at the wrong time was his thing.

It snapped her control though. 'Don't tell me that. You don't know how...It has taken me all this while to adjust to...so don't. Do you know anything about people? About me? What if I go back to what you had made me want to do earlier?'

She remembered wanting to kill herself all the time. To run out into the road and just lie there till a bus found her and crunch-crunched over her. She had promised herself she won't try to kill herself, not until it was really necessary and she could do it right. That is where she craved equality with him, in the matter of life. He was superior to her because he wanted to live and never die until that death came naturally, normally, at the right time in the right way. She scoffed, 'You don't know such simple things about me.'

'You were special,' he said in a rush, careful with the past tense. She had been his exotica, his escape, his getaway, his holiday: that much was true.

'So,' she said, repeating his most recent words. 'I was special.'

Best to go with general, vague terms rather than strong words with negative connotations, nothing to set her off, so he agreed that yes, er, she'd been special.

'Bye,' she said, turning away.

'No. I mean, wait. We haven't decided anything...My mother-in-law was telling me the baby is too far gone to be aborted, that it has to be induced.'

She smiled insolently. 'It is five-thirty, Sam, five-thirty. Time for you to go. Time for me to go.'

And he had actually thought this woman safe. Safe! The laugh was on him. In a spurt of anger, he said, 'You can't just drop a bombshell and...go!'

She looked puzzled. 'You can go back to your life now.'

'Thanks!' She had already turned away from him. 'Why come looking for me if you are so damn organised about things?'

She hesitated. 'I wanted to...nothing.'

'No, tell me,' he said with desperate intensity for a departure from script.

'I wanted, I think, to just see how you feel when you know...'

His face shuttered. Ah, the sadism angle. 'I see,' he nodded, wondering how crass it would be to offer her money instead of pleasantries. Maybe that was the mistake he made in the first place, sweet nothings where some cash would do. He asked, 'When are you planning to leave?'

'Tomorrow.'

Tomorrow was fine, Sam found out. Bilateral talks had broken down, she was going away and having the baby somewhere far away. He felt a mild affection for her, a fondness for her generosity in sweeping his dust under her carpet. He wanted to thank her for not making a nuisance of herself, for going back to the wonder of that first minute of their togetherness when he barely knew her and she him. He wanted to show her the city as he would any outstation acquaintance. 'I wish,' he said and stopped.

'I know,' she said, and their eyes met that way for the very last time.

~

15

On his way back home from the rendezvous with his pregnant ex-girlfriend, Sam waited uneasily for 'tomorrow' like he always did. For her to go back to wherever she came from, for the bombs to stop bubbling up his bloodstream, for his single one-minute extra-marital ejaculation to be filed under Late Lust, for the real job to begin – of placating father-in-law, mother-in-law, probably ex-wife-to-be. What an ex-rated life he was beginning to lead. Damn pheromones! He grinned hysterically at an overtaking driver, flashing him a thumbs-up.

He had totally miscalculated Mira. But how much did anyone know a one-night stand anyway? The chat was nonsensical, geared to break the ice, to advance the game, an excuse to look the merchandise over. But what in the end did one know about another person? The shape of her thighs, sure. The way she came, maybe; the way she came apart, nope. Which was weird when you thought of how much research went into deciding what firm to join, which woman to propose to, when to cross the road, all that looking to the left and looking to the right.

As he turned his car into the road that led to his flat, he expressed concern for himself. The Lalans' car stood outside so no prizes for guessing who sat waiting for him, but his mother being a key member of the mob came as a surprise to Sam.

He put up a hand as if to stem the dissonance. 'I need to eat first,' he said. The nausea had been aggravated by giddiness and he wanted to flush down the bile in his throat. Opening the fridge, taking a couple of eggs out, dicing an onion, adding graying mushrooms. Then a dash into the little storeroom for a quick swig of something to fortify him.

Upon his return to limelight, Sam felt explodable, was careful not to meet any eye. He chewed his omelet along with the eggshells he had accidentally added to it and hoped his babies had eaten today. The mothers seemed too stressed out.

'Ready to kiss and tell?' asked Delta sarcastically when only some flat fragments remained on his plate. Her voice, equipped as it was with the most chalk-on-board gratingness known to human ears, was instantaneously drowned out by the two older women present.

Mrs Lalan and Mrs Shah began to talk at once, drowning out the dramatic import of Delta's query. The gist of their speech consisted of forgiveness, general laments over male foibles, references to recent films on infidelity and, finally, a dissonant homage to Sam's inherent accomplishments. It was clear from their astonished expressions that the two women never meant to defend Sam.

'You have a roving eye!' gasped Delta loudly to hush this double-barreled maternal silliness.

'I don't,' protested Sam conscientiously. 'It roved only *once*.'

'You two-timed.'

'One time.'

'Not chicken-mutton,' added Leela-ben helpfully, 'he is human.'

'What it comes down to is this,' Mr Lalan said to bring some order to the proceedings, 'Are we going to forgive Sam or are we never going to be able to forget?'

Delta glared at her father. His neat little summarisation put the ball in *her* court.

'You are not to get upset,' Sam told his wife in a timid and tender voice. 'You have to think of the baby.'

'What baby?' she lit into him. 'You think on top of all this I will go ahead and have your baby. Let it go, mom,' she said as her mother tried to shush her down with meaningful eye contact.

Mr Lalan started. 'You can't throw away our blood just because...just because this rat ratted on you! I've heard about his father. Always taking the service road when main road is right there. There wasn't a single brothel that he missed and blood will tell, won't it?'

Mrs Shah, unimpressed by Mr Lalan's painstaking research into Sam's family tree, took offence at this brutal dismissal of her late husband. 'Mr Shah was a gem of a person,' she said with all the fervor of a person guilty of not believing in stated facts. 'It is your daughter who is not worthy of my son!'

Sam looked at Delta but she was unreachable. Her chin stuck out in strife, her spine brittled with the effort to contain her rage, her fingers snapped compulsively and her eyes grew glacial. He feared a whole new gamut of hairstyles in the offing.

'Yes, she is going to abort the baby and start a new life. With a decent boy from a decent family.' Mrs Lalan then took out her mobile as if to call up every marriage broker in the vicinity straightaway. She continued to mutter, 'There were boys from America, from Australia...'

'New Zealand,' corrected Mr Lalan, equally angry. 'Not Australia.'

Mrs Lalan did not pause. 'But did she listen? No, only Sam she wanted. He loves me, she kept crying to us, he loves me. Is this what a man in love does to his wife, you tell me. Does he go out and make pregnant the first woman he meets?'

Mrs Shah pointed out that seduction should be added to a young girl's academic syllabus or these things happened.

'You dare to blame it on our daughter?' demanded an incredulous Mr Lalan. 'Here she is in the family way and helpless with an unemployed husband to boot who we now learn sleeps around without a care or...' He stopped as 'condom' was not a word he uttered.

'You are the man she married, okay?' screeched Mrs Lalan, anxious to stress the social favour they had done the lowly Shahs. 'She is the woman supposed to have your babies!'

Delta looked at Sam. Well, she admitted, there were times that that was all Sam was to her, a man she had married whom she as easily may not have married. No, you couldn't say this baby was in any way hers, this new baby, just because Sam was the father. What if she herself had a baby tomorrow? What if Sam wanted yet another baby, whom would he turn to — her or that woman, any woman? What if this encouraged him to sow his wild oats all over the place? Maybe it was addictive to see your sperm sprout hands and legs...

'Beta, pack your bag. Your home is waiting for you,' said Mr Lalan as if it was the most natural thing to say while Mr Lalan squawked that this — where they stood — was their home too as he had paid for it with his own two hands.

'You can't just take her away,' Sam pleaded, his voice high like a woman's, to Mr Lalan. 'She is my wife!' he cried piteously to Mrs Lalan, whose eyes were in the process of their routine widening (her eyes did that come rain or shine, he knew), so that with a sense of failure he turned to Delta, 'I love you!'

'Shut up!' Delta hissed.

'Yes, shut up,' said Leela-ben to Sam. In her time all this love-shuv was restricted to the movies and rightly so. People had no idea how ridiculous the word sounded aloud – love! What did it mean? 'Let them do their worst,' she chided from the sidelines. 'It is not like you lose anything. She takes away this baby, you still have the other baby.'

Mrs Lalan and Delta swiftly glanced at each other. 'She is only one month gone,' said Mrs Lalan, 'we still have time to decide whether we want to keep the baby or not. We will, of course, do what is best for her...and the, er, baby.'

'This baby is ours,' declared Mr Lalan, as if a 50-50 merger had been converted into a takeover. 'You can keep the other.'

Sam stuffed the charred remains of the omelet into his mouth. *Perishables like love and lust were best refrigerated in marriages.* Now that he had beaten his personal famine, he felt woozy in a different way. By the time Delta came down with her chic little trousseau suitcase, he was no longer sure that this was happening, that his pregnant wife was leaving him, that his pregnant mistress was in town, that he was still incredibly hungry, that he suddenly had a craving for kulfi. With tons of rabdi.

'We are going,' announced Mr Lalan to no one in particular and Sam looked at his in-laws. Mrs Lalan's eyes chose that moment to go roaming again. In the space of mere minutes he couldn't take it a second time, no!

'You did it on purpose!' Sam shouted so loudly and so violently that the Lalans left faster than they meant to, not understanding his sudden ire or manner. 'You did it on purpose!' he continued to shout after them.

Delta stood before him, her eyes fixed on him, kohl underlining her disappointment twice over. 'I don't know how to make you happy. I thought I knew. I don't anymore. Bye, Donx.'

He looked at her steadily, putting all his future fidelity and inner purity into that gaze. Minutes ticked by. He knew she would respond, she had to, to such single-minded devotion. She asked, 'So what was it? Long walks on the beach or a bonnet bonk?'

Suddenly he was deadbeat, being a bastard was too much work. 'Bye,' he said, agreeing for now.

He shooed off his mother and wound his way up to his bedroom. Upstairs, he hiccupped and further inebriated himself. There's a womaniser in all men, Sam rationalised. Hetero men wanted harems; monogamy/any-gamy was crap when confronted with the possibility of a lay. Even much-married men – much-married, interestingly, meaning only once married but for an insufferably long time – he knew had their moments of intra-marital lust. Peace was all very well, a given if you did not cross Lakshman rekhas and LoCs, but there was something to bodily good too. Just like the mind could abandon you, leaving you a gibbering idiot who remembers nothing of import on the deathbed, what if the body dumped you first? It was okay to forget every bit of poetry that moved you and even your firstborn's face, but was it okay to puzzle over your own penis, wondering where did it come from, where does it go?

Now if only he could explain all this to wifey dear.

Leela-ben looked at her son with a boys-will-be-boys smile on her face. She had needlessly suspected his manliness, look how he had made her a grandma two times over!

She stroked his hair and, as was her habit at least once a day, mentally reversed to her Republic Day ordeal. 'Pachcha aao,' she had cried out from that hellhole on the fateful day, to whoever went by, to the world, to anyone who could hear and help, to sunshine. 'Come back, come back.' On that eternal night, her body curled within the hardening sludge, incontinent and inconsolable, she thought she had seen 'The End'. Just before she lost consciousness trying desperately to locate light, she had not been calling out to her past recollections alone but also to her future joys. In those last moments of coherence she felt gutted over missing many things down the line, the surprises waiting for her, including the sight, sound and scent of her first grandson.

Leela-ben briskly extracted Mira's whereabouts from Sam. Inadequate nourishment, alcohol on the sly and recent events had enfeebled him enough to readily oblige. His mother said, 'Sleep now, you look tired.'

Grateful for the lack of post-mortems and recriminations, Sam did just that – sleep. Tomorrow Mira would vacate his life and do whatever she wanted with the baby he had never intended to sire. Tomorrow he'd go imploring at the Lalan manor. Tomorrow he'd look around for a job because babies needed funds. Tomorrow there would be no woman named Myrrh…Myrrh? God, what name would a woman named Myrrh choose for her baby? His baby? And how would this his-her baby's mouth get round those oversized nips for a drop of milk? Oh god, it was sure to starve to death! Please let it inherit his lactose intolerance…His brain struggled for a while and then gave up. He snuggled deeper into bed and was fast asleep before he even sniffed the pillow.

Leela-ben spent a minute looking down at him affectionately – two-two kids he had made almost at one go, like twins through different women. An heir and a spare. Her shy little son was growing up! Then she turned to the matter at hand.

From having no grandkids to the prospect of having a pair addled Mrs Shah's sharp mental faculties. Confessing all to Nathu, she shakily bade him to take her to the family's latest bahu.

~

16

Nine p.m. was never less raucous as Mira read out her choices A, B, C and D again. She will go with A. And that is to disappear; easy-peasy as she did not have to disappear per se, only from one person's life.

Her exploits were coming to an end, all that full-throttle frenzy now a small ahem. She imagined Sam lying in his bed wracked with guilt and misgivings – an agreeable image. She had exulted when he earlier sat her down on the broken sofa: *here we go, he is going to bring his First World crisis management to my Third World wreckage.* It did not matter which expression, facial or verbal, was going to denote victor, loser etc and who was anointed what in the end. Somewhere in her where cores were manufactured and set up, she had received a body blow and now she could reassemble again, conduct her own coronation. Relinquish, vanquish, generally shhh…

Being the other, othering, watching him take the high ground – she could not forgive him that. Ever. His being married had catapulted her to the other end of the moral number line. She'd been officially a co-cuckold, consort, concubine, chinna-veedu, however briefly, thanks to him. She had been his grass greener on the other side while he remained the paragon of all virtues for walking away. Sam the Ram.

When, inevitably, he had used the A-word – abortion – she had felt two things. Actually, many things, but chiefly two things. Anger, that he would put out a budding 'them'. And fear, that he could easily find out she had stuffed her clothes, that there was no uterine participation, that the baby was a myth. For all future references called The Myth of Myrrh. Her cigarette-butt soul, which had got used to ashtrays, had begun to smolder once again at such a puff.

In the car on the way here he had spoken little and what he did say she did not listen to. There had been a curious breakdown in the middle of their chat, when he had seemed to speak for her. In a horrible new voice she'd never heard from him he had said, 'You will meet someone who really loves you and whom you really love and you don't want to be held back by this baby that will always remind you of your youthful mistake, do you? Do you? It will spoil your chances in the future with any nice man you might meet…'

Oh, how far removed from the baritone of those goose-pimple days, when it had gone so low, so soft that she had actually felt the words bump against each column of her vertebra. And now they were just guttural thuds. Her eyes had rolled around her head to stop on his face. Pardon? What was he saying? She had felt the way she felt when she sometimes came awake in the middle of a laugh. It would be an uncontrollable, deep gurgle of a laugh, too, disorienting in its heartiness when the sleep had broken, the dream had fled and she was left with the remains of a phantom mirth.

'You mean,' she replied now in the privacy of her room, 'it spoils your future with the nice woman you've already met.'

He was all for taking his disinterest in her and turning it into a....flower! For shaking his head fondly, saying, 'The trouble is, you are not like other women!' Ah, the ultimate charm offensive, she thought in retrospective. After all, which woman craves to be like all the others? She had been busy watching his mouth as it moved, emitting word after word, strung together to form sentences that distanced himself from her in a socially accepted way, with sherbet and pleasantries and the sweet lie of her walking away from him or him dumping her 'for her own good'. The mouth with its previous history of saying the right words, words that had lilted her into verse, the mouth that once brushed against hers and owned her and made her think herself free, free, free to be this mad irresponsible thing like a bird insanely planning to pierce the sky with its tiny little beak.

He had even said something he thought funny. There was that gathering of fine lines around his eyes and mouth. But had she ever found him funny? So funny that she thought she'd fall off her chair or bed or the face of earth? No, she admitted sadly to the pillow that had moved from her belly to the back of her head, your father has no sense of humour.

And no amount of passion, enacted or real, could cure the paucity of laughter. If nothing was absurd and everything awkward, they could explain to themselves the absence of ordinariness between them. They never faked orgasms, only hilarity. There had been no occasion to step straight into his laugh. No ha, ha, ha. Just that un-ha.

If he was to be believed, then this – she – was all wrong for him. Life was so… Panchatantra when you least expect it. She knew there had been no warmth in her eye, smile. But she saw no reason to bring sociability to the table. She wanted to tell him, yes, we are done. And the good news was it will never happen to her again. The bad news, however, was she could barely listen to anybody's love story – the magical beginning, the accidental rubbing of their body parts in public, their birth control methods – without puking right into their mouths.

Bye, bye, Sam. She had done her time in cotton candy land, had cut through the *panjaara adi*, fought the sugar jungle, the cloying stickiness of it. Mira felt a new type of tears spring to her eyes, of joy, for herself, for all this fount of wisdom. Where was the champagne? Where was at least the sweet lime soda? Suddenly she was giddy with relief. No more drama queen, no more pillow on person. She wanted to shout from the rooftops that she had a flat, really flat, stomach under all that sponge. She felt…restored.

Yes, she had crawled out from under a rock, but creepy-crawlies have rights too. She was on the world's stage, surrounded by the rejected, the dejected, the ejected. She was at a romantic candlelight dinner for one. After all, if two people can locate their mouths by candlelight, so could one.

The thought of food was agreeable after a long, long time. Tastes crowded her tongue, manna filled her mouth. She was thinking of prawns and squids and newborn sardines fried to a crisp when she heard the knock.

Someone at the door. Sam! Back to grovel at her feet. She wheezed, looking at the window. No, too high to jump out. Where on earth was the bump? Mira scrambled to her feet, abandoning global glory for a mad search for the truant cushion and finally locating it right where her head had been resting. She was a mite irritated. It was like ever since she met Sam, an extortionist lurked at her door, her bed, the corner of her eye, demanding she pay up or else.

Moments later, her abdomen levitating, she opened the door with some semblance of sanity...to an old woman she'd never met.

'Myself Sam's mommy.'

~

17

'You are Sam's baby's mommy, no? When is the due date?'

Mira polished her subtraction skills – nine minus six – and picked a date associated with children, 'November 14.'

'Just three months away! You could go into labour in the seventh month. What do doctors know? They are no dai. A dai can just place her hand on the stomach and predict boy or girl, today or tomorrow, head-first or breech. Everything okay otherwise?'

Mira nodded cautiously, paling at the thought of her 'bump' being manhandled.

'When was the last scan?'

'Last week?' Mira hazarded a guess.

'Must move a lot, nathi?'

'Not much,' hedged Mira warily.

'Now I am going to scold you,' warned Leela-ben, face wreathed in good intentions. 'I am sure you have not told your mother about the baby. I am right, no? I am the baby's other grandmother and have every right to scold you for risking its life this way. Don't you know better than to drop from the skies one fine day and say I am pregnant. That too to a married man! You know how angry that can make the man's wife and her side of the family?'

Mira nervously swallowed some necessary spittle. She imagined the Lalans and their precious darling daughter waiting outside with rifles and an axe. For some reason she had always thought axe murderers more murderous than shooters – they so seemed to relish the personal contact.

'From now on until you have the baby I am your mother, like it or not. Your baby will come much before Delta's anyway, so we do not have to worry. Hers may come or not, what's it to us?'

'She is expecting?' asked Mira faintly.

'Can you imagine? I'd like to see a healthy baby squeeze past those hips. Why do you think the Taj Mahal's four pillars are set wide apart? So the Taj has enough space to breathe, that is why. Anyway, look at me, sitting here talking away like a foolish old woman. Pack your bags quickly and settle your bill here, Sam is waiting for us.'

It took only words on Leela-ben's part to conclude the deal her way. Mira pointed out that her ticket was already booked, that she had to rejoin work – a statement that almost earned her a slap from Sam's mother, there was to be no more working it seemed – and that she had a million chores waiting for her in the form of her previous and real life, but the older woman just clucked and clucked.

Mira saw she had no choice. 'You are being so nice,' she said softly, still baffled by the maternal invasion. 'Am I not the enemy?'

Mrs Shah tossed back her thin plait. 'Enemy hamare dushman!'

Mira sat in the car, where the strangeness of her life continued to play itself out. Outside, people moved to the left or right, talking animatedly, walking their dog, eating bhel. It seemed so long ago that she had stood amidst her own leftovers, tossing a mental coin whether to keep or bin. And it seemed even longer ago that she had contemptuously sized up her mother's multi-shelved, spice-stained kitchen and sworn never to duplicate it. She had stood in small geometrically measurable sunlit spots and contemplated remote issues like political coups in foreign countries, bored in a delicious way. And now all was soap opera.

To be escorted with such gentleness and deposited at the journey's end right in Sam's bed was to have her dreams and nightmares meet in a road crash. Mira soon found herself lying within touching distance of Sam on wheat-coloured, starch-smelling sheets with the door firmly locked behind Mrs Shah's back, who went away with the unintentionally menacing whisper, 'I am right outside the door if you need anything.'

En route Mrs Shah had enquired about her food cravings, her blood group, her family's medical history, including dental records, her former relationships if any, and a dazed Mira had tried her best to be truthful. She had even managed a horrified murmur against stretching out on Sam's conjugal bed, but Mrs Shah brushed aside her protests. 'If you can have his baby, you can sleep in his bed. It is time he enjoyed the company of a real woman for a change.'

So a night that Mira had thought to dedicate to imaginary applause and deep, refreshing sleep after her avenging act transformed into long unending hours of chronic insomnia when she had no choice but to rehash her Mata Hari moment and register Sam's wife's skills at interior decoration. Biblical mix-ups were depicted in large, sweeping strokes on the walls. Eve tossed auburn curls over her shoulder and grinned at Adam. A badly drawn serpent raised what looked like a grocery bag for hood. Apples in impossible red, flowers in unseasonal bloom, fawns a startled beige: Eden overdone in every painting.

She looked around cautiously, ordering her brain to stop rat-nibbling into her thoughts. *This is Sam's house. This is Sam's bedroom. This is Sam's bed. And this,* she glanced at him again, *is Sam.* Not photo or fancy, but in person. Breathing and snoring and making little snuffling noises with his head buried under the white mountainous pillow of impossibly frilly lace. She checked for bodily fluids. Nah, watertight.

Over the course of the next seven hours, the interloper lay revising her actions so far, berating herself, recognising the precarious position she was in and bitterly regretting her immodesty once upon a time. Vague longings were the worst, she conceded. Would she one morning wake up cured of him or did she need the addiction more than she needed him and therefore never be cured? Wherefrom did this certainty spring? That there was something here to dig and delve into, like gold buried long ago, waiting for her to arrive to once again glitter in the light.

What had she come for?

Going by her gut instinct, Mira had searched her mother's cupboard and found them, her beloved dolls. Her best ones – Sara, Gina and the petite one, Sarla. The one she loved the most had gone missing for always though. Into some netherland of dead dolls. Her mother had explained patiently and angrily and with father for witness that she meant no harm, that it was just high time Mira gave up playing with dolls, that was all. That people were talking, that there were rumours of madness. That if she wanted, it was technically time for her to have her own babies and give up all this nonsense about dolls. That this was all for her good, believe it or not.

Mira had stared at her mother incredulously and cried for a long time, but the longer she cried, the longer they were convinced of what they had done. It had to be stopped, she had to grow up and get on with life. She was sixteen for God's sake, how long was she going to comb synthetic hair on little doll heads? Mira couldn't sleep at nights, thinking they were calling out to her, whimpering, all her mutilated doll darlings. Her semi-people, her people in practice. They had been good girls, her dolls, until their grandma went nuts on them...

Mira tossed and turned all night, restless under the covers, between faith and faithlessness, recalling each doll, their little faces molded in expressions of eternal trust, Sam's lies, her own lies. Why? For what?

For what? They kept you sane, little girl, they kept you going! They kept you from you and all that loneliness away. Stopped your clock-watching, got you from point A to point B, to this precise moment in time when you mockingly ask them what did they do for you. Lies are truth before their time, lies are truth in waiting, giving the truth time to ripen and be ready for the tongue's plucking.

Everything that happens in life happens only to kill time? I don't believe it! All that I hold dear, all my loving and hating, my possessions, my jealousies, they are just, what, distractions?

Breaking gently to you, in bits of so-called lovingness, the unloveability of you! You give and you take nothing, you partake of zilch, but the elaborateness of the ruse entertains the eye and the ear. You are so busy thinking and feeling and spinning this way and that, that you get away from you. You can't deny that.

No, she couldn't, more's the pity. At a gray moment in early a.m. Mira cautiously slipped out of bed to go to the adjoining loo. Here she readjusted the cushion against her belly, brushed her teeth with toothpaste on a finger and sipped tap water.

Sam, still in bed, heard the flush and thought it must be at least ten if Delta was up. He rolled over when he heard her coming back to show off his first erection of the day resurrecting softly from its cotton shroud in all its morning glory.

'It's me,' said Mira tentatively. Oh, the ignominy of being wanted so rampantly so wrongly!

Sam jackknifed in bed blinking multiple times, but no, the apparition did not move away or betray any tendency to vaporise. 'You are stalking me,' he stated matter-of-factly, gathering the sheets primly over his lower half, where wilt had set in. 'Did you get in through the window?'

An accusation Mira could not deny in all fairness, seeing she must appear like a home-delivery booty call. So she opted for the more recent truth, of his mother descending on her, dragging her here against her will etc with the fervent hope in her heart that he would at least now play hero and come charging to rescue her from the nightmare of herself.

'You could have said no,' wailed Sam, eyes full of early morning matter and earnestness.

'Yes,' Mira agreed. She should have said no right from the start itself. *No to you, no to me, no this egoistic prank, no to instant stardom.* She opened the door wide to let in fresh air and...Mrs Shah.

'Slept well?' asked a beaming Leela-ben, bearing a tray with tea for her son and a glass of warm milk with honey and saffron for the new member of the family carrying within her the newest member of the family. Having rummaged through Mira's bags for iron tablets – the most skin-darkening agent known to man – last evening while they packed, she had been reassured by its absence. Doctors will say eat iron, it is somebody else's baby, na?

There followed a barrage of Gujarati words between mother and son, the gist of which was clear to Mira by the emphatic gesturing in her direction by Sam and the soothing tones employed by Mrs Shah. Suddenly Sam clutched at his hair and sank into bed with a keening cry. Bewildered, Mira looked at the other woman.

'I told his wife, that's all,' she shrugged. 'I told his wife that you are now here to take care of Sam, a job she should be doing.'

Before Mira could apply herself to this new development, Sam jumped out of bed and began to run around the room, picking up each object, muttering, 'My phone, my phone.'

Mira picked up her own, went to 'Contacts' and pressed Littleshit under L. Nothing rang anywhere in the room.

He straightened. 'Oh, it is in my pants.' And got it from the trouser pocket hanging on the back of a chair.

'You changed your number?' asked Mira, sounding totally betrayed for the first time.

'That was my office mobile, I returned it to them,' he mumbled.

The…little shit, she fumed, watching him agitatedly push open the balcony door and speak into the phone. All those messages she had sent him pouring her heart out and saying she would kill herself – he hadn't even bothered to get them!

'Drink the milk,' Mrs Shah said kindly.

Mira gulped the milk down in one warm swallow. 'Good girl,' approved Mrs Shah, removing her statuesque frame from the room.

In the kitchen she briskly chopped up fruits into a tangy chaat to beguile Mira's taste-buds. The poor thing had such a lost look, like Leela-ben herself when she had first met Sam's father's family. Leela-ben shuddered. She had never forgotten what it had felt to be so alone, and then later, even more alone, eyes and ears sealed by rubble, mouth screaming mud. Her mantra had been simple then − let me live, let me live, letmelive. That was what this baby was saying to her now, 'Let me live'.

Leela-ben baby-talked with an inward suck of her lips. 'Dadi is here, you are safe,' she crooned, searching frantically for chaat masala in Delta's hip but hopeless kitchen.

~

18

Mira looked uncertainly at Sam's silhouette, which managed with its slumped shoulders and general slant to eloquently convey despair through the curtain. Not wanting him to think her an eavesdropping voyeur on top of being a gatecrasher, she started to aimlessly walk around the room, playing tourist, looking at the bric-a-brac, the jumble of curios. Only then did she notice the tiny brushstroke at the bottom corner of the awful Eden paintings: *Sam*. She felt a moment of unease. The wife, Delta, was slowly beginning to step out of the fog. She was a woman who put aside her own taste — any taste, really — to put *this* up on the wall only because her husband had caused it.

Mira took off for a longish bath to erase the embarrassment of being in such a pioneering position. Also, the skin under the cushion was itching up a storm. She took as long as she could, but when her skin began to shrivel and match the colour of her lips under the gush of hot water, she decided to unfold the large towel on the rack. A fresh one. A used one hung on the hook behind the door, but she was not tempted to rub Sam's used towel against her skin. That wouldn't be romantic, that would be retarded.

Strapping the cushion back into place like an armament before battle, she prepared to go back into the bedroom. After all, he had just woken up, not brushed his teeth etc. She took a lingering look at the mirror, *his* mirror, a mirror that had reflected him so many times…'Shut up,' snarled her image. And she scooted out.

At first she thought she had the room to herself for there was no sign of Sam. But then she spotted him, lying in an unnatural position in the balcony. He had died! She had finished him off. Her lies, her foolish tit for tat had killed him. But I did not know his wife was pregnant, she tried to pep-talk herself out of the panic. Where was that dumb woman who had airlifted her here?

Leela-ben rushed up at first cry, saying, 'Don't come down the stairs in your condition, I am coming up. What, what do you want?' She panted by the door and then looked past Mira at a supine Sam on the balcony floor.

'It is a heart attack,' said the doctor in an irritated voice. Being harassed simultaneously by two women was no picnic. 'We need to shift him to a hospital right now. I have called for an ambulance.'

'We cannot wait for ambulance-shambulance,' cried Leela-ben, stopping herself in the nick of time from hitting the doctor on the side of his head. 'We will carry him down to my car. My driver can help.'

'We'll be just two of us,' began the doctor, taking in Leela-ben's advanced age and Mira's telltale bulge.

'We can carry him down,' echoed Mira in a higher pitch, eyes still on Sam. *Have I cursed him too much? Brought him down with my pull in the celestial world?* Somehow she'd gotten into the wrong queue and applied for a passport to hell. Would she now have to watch her first love draw his last breath?

'Not in your condition,' averred Leela-ben. 'The three of us can manage.' She called out in ear-splitting volume. 'Nathu!'

'This? Don't mind this,' said Mira, patting her stomach.

'Of course, I will mind it, silly girl. We don't need two-two crises on our hands, do we?'

'I am not pregnant.'

'You are emotional,' said Leela-ben and told the doctor authoritatively, 'Pregnant women are emotional.'

Exasperated, Mira tugged under her chest and with a soft plop out fell the cushion between her feet. 'There's no baby, Mrs Shah.' She was bleached of all colour, almost albino, but her hands already supported Sam's shoulders without waiting for the others to get into action.

Tipping a limp Sam onto a beanbag and helping to drag it out by the lift, Mira went back into the house to hunt for lock and key as Mrs Shah, floundering under the fear of losing only son after the brutal loss of an imminent grandson, was in no fit condition to be consulted. And it was here while looking around for lock and key that Mira began to gauge the depth of her idiocy. Behind the framed photographs of the happy couple, under the coir mats and in drawers galore, Mira found not just the lock and key but the shared lifetime of another people. It was like prying into strangers' things in the aftermath of a tragedy and finding possessions familiar for their wear and tear yet unfamiliar for belonging to others. The guilt was excruciating. She tapped right into the rich vein of right-wing Christian conscience.

Mira was just about to close the door when she spied the cushion lying forlorn on the floor. She picked it up, it could support Sam's head.

Nobabynobaby went Leela-ben's mind like a ghostly typewriter banging on the same keys, but she was galvanised into action, propping her son, lifting him partially along with the others as they went down the front steps to the car.

'Nathu,' she ordered, 'put Sam in the front.'

This confused everybody else, no matter how well-acquainted they were with Leela-ben's eccentricities. 'Better to put him in the backseat, so he can stretch out,' suggested the doctor disinterestedly.

'Aha, and kill him?' Leela-ben asked. 'My husband died in the backseat. Accident. I don't want a truck to kill Sam off!'

Somehow they wedged Sam horizontally into the front-seat along with Nathu. The doctor, who was adjusting Sam from one door, looked up and met the cleavage of Mira, who was arranging Sam from the opposite door. 'I think I will come to the hospital, after all,' he began to insist.

'No need,' said Leela-ben, 'You are not cardiologist, no?'

'I'm thinking of MD-ing in it. And I can help,' he smiled at Mira intimately, 'fill forms at the reception.'

Mira smiled back, flustered. 'Get in,' Leela-ben told Mira and Mira stopped smiling and got in. But not before the doctor gave her a handshake that was firm, yes, clinical, no.

Once Nathu stepped on the gas, Mrs Shah began to talk...to God. Mrs Shah's prayers were in vernacular but Mira could make out the urgency in her bargaining. 'Please,' she found herself praying too. 'Please God, make her wish come true, whatever it is.' There was such raw and naked pain in the other woman's voice, Mira couldn't bear her own crookedness anymore. She was being sucked into a situation beyond her control. Agreed, she had come here to get her own way, to scare Sam senseless, but scaring him to death would be taking things too far. She had no choice, however much it went against her principles to hang around the man who broke her heart and inspired such heights of malevolence in her, but to see it through.

Briefly Sam regained consciousness, but his brief interlude of lucidity escaped the rapidly praying women. He found himself crumpled in the car's front-seat, the pain traveling through his chest faster this way. His abdomen contorted, feet in Nathu's lap and head on a cushion, Sam shut his eyes against the flickering lights from the moving window. 'I am dying, I am dying,' he thought with his usual flair for theatrics.

I will never see my children, he thought next with great sadness. Not that he had thought of kids in the conventionally joyous way until now. To Sam, there had been something vacuous in wanting kids without rhyme or reason. If Delta had put out welcome mats on the right parts of her body at the right time, he wouldn't even have tried to dangle the baby bait. Sure, people regenerated, but there was a mindless quality to it. In his opinion far too many were wont to lisp for babies in a fit of vanity. Riding in the car, listening to two women worry loudly about his health and doubt his posterity, Sam confessed readily to himself his earlier non-fascination with kids. He used to find babies creepy, the way they met your eyes without saying a word. Once a baby had smiled at him, revealing its only tooth. Oh yes, babies could be sinister.

But when Delta told him she was expecting, Sam's cover had been blown. He stood revealed as a man like any other man who was pathetic enough to want a clone or human memento to leave behind when he died. And now, just when he thought his life to be the one that he wanted to be living, things had gone haywire thanks to his truly. When Delta called up to say, 'Sam, I am lying in the hospital bed and right now, this minute, they are killing our baby and it is all your fault,' everything had gone black.

And remembering the moment that everything went black, everything went blessedly black once more.

In the hospital, a flurry of activity busied both the women: filling forms, listening apprehensively to the white-coat men with their stethoscopes, watching nurses tug at the stretcher that carried an unconscious Sam away from them into a world of electric shocks and surgical instruments and beeping waves on multi-coloured machines.

'He is only thirty-seven,' Leela-ben told the nurse sadly. 'And he is not overweight, never drank or smoked. All this is too much shock for him, he's always been a weak boy. First the baby, add one baby, minus one baby. I remember when he was five…'

Mira cut through this potted history, finding that she herself had no interest in Sam's childhood antics, to say, 'Don't we have to call up his wife?'

'That…child? What will she do? She is the one who's given him this heart attack in the first place. You had not told him that there was no baby, na? He must have fallen at her feet over the phone, she must have repeated whatever her mother told her to say, that she will kill the baby. I tell you, continuous cutting of hair can affect the brain!'

Mutely Mira shook her head. She was blameless in certain respects it would seem.

Mrs Shah opened her voluminous bag and took out the squashed looking cushion she had rescued from the car. 'Sam's system can't take a second shock right now. You need to stay pregnant or *you* will be the one to kill him.'

In the hospital's loo, Sam's mother made a compact bump under Mira's loose top. If at all Mira had gotten down to mull it over, Sam's mother would have been only one more person to hate. She is the one, Mira would've presumed, who taught him in childhood, 'Done with your toys? Throw them away.' But watching the woman's tongue protrude in her effort to smooth any lumps, Mira felt mellow. 'I mean,' she said to herself, 'she is not someone I am allowed to like or dislike, but…'

'Enough,' said Leela-ben to still her own compulsive smoothening of cushion, but stemming Mira's disjointed recycling of guilt.

Regardless of Leela-ben's efforts to shush up the matter, a delicate network of Gujju medicos carried the news to Delta's ears and within an hour of Sam's admittance, the corridor outside the ICU was filled with the entire Lalan clan. A doctor came out and announced that Sam had passed the cardiac crisis, though he did not rule out the possibility of after-shocks. When Mr Lalan swept into the corridor, Mrs Shah forgot, and perhaps forgave, all former jibes against her men-folk and ran up to him with tidings of joy. 'He is fine now, fine now! I prayed to his father's soul and the miracle happened.'

'Remarkable,' said Mr Lalan after a small pause that was open to interpretation. However, his credit card and connections were unequivocal and soon had the doctors file in with minute to minute medical bulletins, which though repeats, calmed Leela-ben's birdlike breast.

By evening most of the people bearing the Lalan name, including Mr Lalan, departed for home. Some of the Lalans wondered over their *theplas* and sweet mango chutney later: 'Who was that pregnant woman, by the way? Never seen her before.'

Mrs Lalan sat on the left side of the corridor with her daughter on a hastily procured bench. On the right side were Mrs Shah and Mira on chairs that were already there, staking prior claim. And from these opposite ends, they faced each other like wrestlers with their managers. The older women continued with their cold war and no one bothered to introduce the younger women.

Every time Delta studied Mira, the latter studied the floor. When Mira studied Delta, the latter returned the compliment. In such judicious manner did Delta celebrate Mira's matted hair that canceled out the bigness of her breasts. *So this is my husband's type.*

Delta, meanwhile, was breaking news on Mira.com. Hmmm, thought Mira, if Sam was husband, here was vice-versa. Delta was beautiful in a misshapen sort of way. A designer gypsy with subtle gums and cheekbones slanting like ski slopes in foreign calendars. But something about Delta's face gouged the eye: perhaps the black gloss on bee-stung lips, the belligerent kohl tattooed under her eyes or the hair nailed to the high forehead in a bold fringe. Her slight build and baggy clothing made for indistinct gender, while Mira's love handles alone accounted for Delta's total BMI. Physically, Mira was half a dozen Deltas.

Earlier on, during a lull when Mr Lalan organised tea for everyone, Mrs Shah had leaned over to whisper, 'Don't say anything about the baby yet.' Which reminded Mira that the cushion was still among them.

And now Delta's eyes flickered over the cushion, naturally. Since the cushion forced her thighs apart, Mira was dying to cross her legs. Of course, if she had kept her legs wisely crossed six months ago, she wouldn't be here at all on an uncomfortable aluminum chair, watching accident victims being brought in with bleeding heads and smashed ribs, and smelling antiseptic smells. Not a happy place to be. Not a happy place at all.

Mrs Shah kept one hand firmly on Mira's stomach. Mira knew why: she could feel the other woman's elderly fingers try to smoothen, smoothen constantly. 'The baby,' Mrs Shah muttered. 'They poke out all the time, all elbows and knees.'

Delta seemed obsessed by her sneakers. To be fair, they looked new.

By and by, Mrs Lalan and Mrs Shah began to nod off sleepily. Soon they were fast asleep, waking up only when their lolling heads jerked their necks painfully. Then they'd blink owlishly, declare loudly that they were not sleeping – far from it, really – and slowly begin to nod off again. Mrs Lalan waved a hand in her sleep, saying, 'Puppa, puppa!'

Exchange of involuntary smiles between the younger women. Mira raised a hesitant hand, brought it parallel to her ear and waved. Delta, armpits dead from weight training the whole morning, nodded back. Heartbreak always had her hit the gym.

Mira, though charlatan, knew that words were necessary. 'I shouldn't be here.'

'You did what you had to do,' pacified Delta, beatific from fatigue and shock. 'You have to tell the father you are having his baby.'

'I am not.'

'You feel like that now. Wait until all this is over. Then you'll be glad at least you have this baby.'

'How can you say that when you know the baby almost killed Sam?'

'Oh no, you can't take all the credit, you know. He collapsed while talking to *me*, after I banged the phone down on him. It is me who almost killed him, not you. I told him I got rid of the baby. That's what gave him the heart attack. I shouldn't be telling you this but,' she shrugged, 'I have to tell someone.'

The confession jolted through Mira like hasty liquor, watering her eyes and bringing up her breath in a cough. For a while she continued to be in this dim-lit corridor, inspiring confidences, doling out absolutions. Then she thought, this woman is lying. Between last night and this morning where was the time for her to consult a doc, let alone execute a murder, however nascent? Oh Sam, your baby is intact. All this melodrama for nothing.

'Anyway, between us, we'll be giving him a baby, won't we?' Delta said.

Had she guessed the truth of her non-baby? Was the cushion giving itself away? Mira surreptitiously looked down. 'I am sorry,' began Mira, but Delta cut in, 'Just go have the baby somewhere. If you intend to give it for adoption,' she shrugged again, 'give it to us.'

'You can forget this baby. Pretend I never came here, pretend I never said I am carrying.'

'And what will we say to make him *live*? Where's the baby we can hold up for him to see?'

'You mean, you really had an abortion...?'

'I swear on Sam's head, I have no baby on me.' Delta stood up.

Mira at once noticed the basic difference between her and Sam's wife – grace. When Delta sat or stood, it was a movement of decision and economy, and she caught admiring looks like dry tinder the match. Mira was reminded of a little ceramic swan she had once seen in a shop.

Between the two of them, Mira had to admit, it was she, beefy and burly, who would always look pregnant. Not Delta, who had the magic of light bones.

19

Mrs Shah patted her plait, pleased to be the first one to be allowed into Sam's presence. Upon her return the others fell on her. How is he, is he conscious, did he recognise you, did he say anything, did he ask about me... Questions to which Mrs Shah gave noncommittal replies, taking her cue from Sam's shut-eyed silence.

The four women had been shooed out of the corridor early dawn as the hospital was expecting an inspection team from the state government. Unable to book a room in the premises – 'They are saying ICU patients won't get rooms as they are already occupying ICU,' said Leela-ben – they went along to the common bathroom where unlatched doors necessitated a sorority of sorts with each guarding the door while the other went in.

They then gravitated towards the hospital cafeteria where Delta soberly owned up to her part in the current crisis. Mrs Shah patted her cheek. 'Don't worry, beta,' she said, more anxious about her son than prospective grandsons right now, 'Some people are not meant to have a baby. That's nothing to be ashamed about.'

Mrs Lalan was trying Mr Lalan's number at that moment – she felt duty-bound to fill up her husband's cellphone with missed calls from her in her spare time as an indication of her 'caring' – and missed this potentially explosive remark.

On a medicine-purchase errand a short while later, Delta fished out blueberry sauce-coated small change from a denim pocket, saying, 'This is your first baby.'

The absence of a question mark allowed Mira some respite, but she had a job not sizing up the various brands of sanitary napkins on the chemist's counters.

Delta said with a wobble in her voice, 'Please, please, don't let anything happen to this baby. That will finish Sam off.'

Mira took a deep breath, nodded. Because she did not want to finish off this woman. As they walked back, Mira dragged her feet and watched the bony arch of Delta's body. Mira rubbed her hands, there went her chances of having a convenient 'miscarriage' in a week or two.

'I might as well have the baby,' she thought glumly and waddled after Delta.

~

20

Two days later Sam was shifted to a private room, which was almost like a suite on Mr Lalan's insistence.

Mr Lalan had figured out a fundamental lesson about father-in-lawing from recent events: estranged sons-in-law brought mud to family name, but dead sons-in-law ended the family name. Better for the bloke to live on gibbering about paintbrushes than to have to organise funeral, attendant rituals and ceremonies and annual grinning photo in newspapers and embarking on the tiresome process of settling only daughter all over again with, in all probability, a bigger idiot.

Mr Lalan pressed an add-on credit card into his wife's hand and disappeared into his dogs and TV debates on global warming.

In the inner room lay the patient, slowly coming back to life with the added complication of high diabetes brought on by severe stress and in the outer room, the one with the TV set and mini refrigerator, were Delta and Mira, newbie roomies. They had persuaded the older women to go back home and get some rest. Mrs Shah obeyed after a while, thinking, soon the doctors will allow Sam to eat what he wants, then I can make him stuff he likes at home. He had been eating Delta's errors or their cook's idea of edible fare until recently and for now the hospital menu ruled.

'Donx,' cried Delta demonstratively when the three of them were alone.

Mira watched as 'Donx' opened his eyes in slits and closed them again. She remembered him telling her with that killer smile of his in the Bangalore office a lifetime ago that his name was Sam. Even then he had been some other woman's property; he had pretended to be her Sam all the while that he was somebody else's something else. And how she had hated – with what bloodcurdling name-calling – Samundar Shah, a man whose real name had only been an alias. She should have known, every man was some other woman's Donx.

Delta patted his hand, the one that lay outside the covers, question mark on her face, asking, 'Do you know who I am?' and he shook his head in 'I don't know'.

Mira watched as Delta held on – just about – to her calm, knew that they were unfortunately the three words most likely to take a loved one by the throat and rattle like a kitten in a dog's mouth. Mira knew exactly how Delta felt, for hadn't she herself been his Idon'tknow for so long, till she came here and plonked herself in his path and damaged his heart as physically as he had damaged hers emotionally?

When the doctor called 'wife of patient' in for a talk, Delta looked pleadingly at Mira, so that they both walked into the room together, ready to face the medical crux of the matter in newfound sisterhood.

The doctor, unsure about the real Mrs Shah, disseminated knowledge evenly to the two anxious women before him. 'Your husband has suffered acute myocardial infarction, or AMI, what we call a heart attack. Blood supply to the heart was blocked and some heart cells were given the pink slip.' Here he smiled, causing the two women to smile back automatically. He then lapsed back into professional jargon, more to downplay the seriousness of what happened as, in his experience, women were quick to lose composure and disorderly women did nothing for his peace of mind or hospital decorum.

Delta and Mira flinched at the rain of words. Coronary artery, vulnerable atherosclerotic plaque, macrophages, ischemia...Such calm consonants on their own but so menacing together. When they came out of the room, Mira and Delta did not speak but walked close together.

Speech was banned so Sam could only blink at his erstwhile paramour and current spouse – both, of course, livid with him if memory served him right – cozily alternating chores between them.

Right now right here his gratitude was solely reserved for life itself. He was alive! The pressing pain, the nausea, the sweating, the palpitations, the death bugle were all gone. When the symptoms first hit him, he had thought that keeping his stomach empty for too long the previous day had given him gas. And since indigestion could easily pass off for the soul's mutterings, he had blamed future fatherhood twice over, meeting up with a misplaced mistress and being read the riot act by wronged wife for the shooting pains in his chest. To think he had been actually having a heart attack! That right now he could be warming a funeral pyre!

Delta scurried about lithely, maintaining at all times only a specious eye contact, as if she wanted to ensure that he did not go wanting for anything, but surely, he thought, more to strengthen his shame, lest he forget his trespasses against her.

And his little Mirabai? Who had travelled far to pin him down. She fumbled about the place, too late or too early with whatever was required – sentences or spoon. Her eyes downcast, demure as a new bride. Starting if he so much as glanced at her, making his eyes as jumpy as her nerves in turn. Given a chance, he knew she'd gather him to her and burp him like a baby. The heart attack had gotten everyone on his side, except of course good health.

And though he lay there so still, Sam knew he occupied only the space he immediately did in his physical capacity as a body, that he owned no real estate in their hearts at the moment. They were just three people shuffling around to make space for each other. They looked at him, he knew. They looked at him caringly, much too often and listeningly. And he resented that they could look at him and he couldn't look at them. That they had the advantage of clean eyes. Clean, uncheating eyes.

He lay still, very vegetable, focused on recouping strength, passionately missing what bodies were capable of, the energy, the sheer fizz of functional knees, limbs, elbows and wrists. Souls got all the press but bodies have a language too. Sam sighed: heart attacks made a Buddha out of anyone.

Mira hid behind a magazine as Delta sponge-bathed her husband. The body of Sam as she had seen long ago was now the body of Sam as she never wanted to see it. It flipped and it flopped and was as helpless as a newborn's but with all the klutziness of the post-pubertal distances it had traveled. She occasionally read out from the mag – a showbiz divorce was the cover story – to entertain Delta and to prove that she was indeed reading and not eyeballing her yester-beau.

'You know that's all crap, that men know when their wives are sleeping around or that women know when men are having an affair. There is no sixth sense about these things, just the damn lipstick on the collar. My intuition doesn't work that way. I can't ask it anything. It tells me.'

And though Mira busily flipped pages, flap-flap, she was impressed enough to change messiahs on the spot. Delta reminded her of her various aunts and grandaunts who fed their husbands beef and pork and rabbit and duck from day one and bumped them off early with cholesterol and now lived alone in their huge rose-ringed bungalows and giggled through church-planned trips to the Holy Land every year with other Syrian Christian widows. There was that same invisible party hat on Delta's head.

The evening brought a visitor: the doctor who had helped with Sam at his flat on the day of the heart attack. It was soon apparent whom he had really come to see. After a perfunctory glance at Sam and a glassy-eyed reception to Delta's breathless recounting of medical facts so far, he turned with great familiarity, hands curbed in pant pockets, to Mira. 'And?'

In the silence that followed, Sam and Delta looked at Mira first with faint surprise, then at each other with a measure of understanding. Though Mira dug a toe into the frayed carpet, the doctor persevered, his bias for her apparent. 'Your husband is OK now,' he reassured, flashing the same intimate smile he had flashed her on the heart-attack morning. A smile so practised, he could

157

smile no other way. From his patients to his Pomeranian, all were recipients of this sudden sensuousness.

Delta cut in haughtily, 'My husband.'

The doctor, who had taken Delta to be Sam's sister because of the generic resemblance and her lack of adipose like the patient, looked at Mira, who nodded.

'Why don't you two go for a walk?' suggested Delta.

Only slightly alarmed, Mira walked around the hospital gardens with ...?

'Amit,' he said and launched into predetermined banter, which, like good Bollywood fare, had a little of everything – pathos, song, villain and punch-lines. She laughed in the right places, at least what she hoped were right places, pleased to listen.

'OK,' he said eventually, 'do you, like, have someone?'

Mira thought hard. And decided that she did not, like, have someone. But before she could articulate this newfound lack, he nodded. 'OK,' he said again, apparently at a loss to replace words, 'OK. I just thought, you know, now that I know you are not married...'

'No, no, I am glad you came to say hello,' she said.

'I was going to ask you if you usually fool your mother-in-law with a cushion up your dress, but she is not your...'

'Yeah, she is not.'

'And he is not your...'

She shook her head and then thought she should clarify further, though she knew not why. Maybe because she was hanging around in said man's sickroom, ostensibly tending to his needs. How could she say, 'If he dropped dead and was devoured by rabid dogs I would not want to know', without sounding like, 'damn, I care'? I was causing his possible death, not his death per se that she cared about. Also, it was too early to tell this new man – with whom it'd probably be too early all her life – that if it was him under attack by the same dogs, she might try to get a cat from nearby to distract the dogs. Because he may ask, 'That is it?????' Anything she said may be held against her. Moody bastards, words.

Silence stretched from the sparse, carefully cultivated shrubbery around them to the cafeteria nearby and the doctors' colony further away, and in the comfort of such stillness he took his leave and she watched him walk away, this Amit, feeling like she'd passed a test with flying colours.

~

21

Sam had started to talk, inaudibly and to himself. His mother, when she came visiting, shoved her ear close to his mouth and pretended he was talking sense and happily interpreted his sibilant exhalations any which way she saw fit. 'He wants hot water for his feet,' she'd say, jumpstarting Delta into scurrying for hot water and towel-draping his feet.

Mira's continued presence panicked Sam only mildly. On the whole, he was relieved that she was out in the open, her belly on show, so that he could apologise, say sorry in the right quarters and get on with life. Also, what did offspring, however illegitimate they may be, matter in the face of death? But Delta...he was infinitely grateful for her attentions, for her continual occupation of their coupledom. For being there for him. Wasn't that what commitment was about? Just being there. Anyone could stray. But could everyone stick around?

Sensing an impending attack of the maudlin, he quickly detoured to couples in general, thinking how no one could make sense of successful alliances between man and woman. Why did they come together? Why did they go on after bombings and battles? And the more mismatched a pair appeared to the eye, the more they went on, he observed sagaciously.

He thought of this woman he used to know. What was her name, yes, Tara. One fine day someone told him, Tara is marrying Basu, did you know, and he had gone, shit, how come I missed the entire drama of them. Men and women met all the time of course. It was funny how they found each other somehow. And at the moment it felt like such an absolute knowing, like the instinctive knowledge of the edge of the bed that one never rolled off. There really is nothing written in the stars, no pairs foretold.

People just ran into each other because they simply couldn't sit at home all day. They paid fake compliments, smoked and coughed and laughed delightedly at bad jokes. Then, at some point, all of society needed to be pared down to one. Someone to take home and screw the hell out of. Well, thought Sam, every organ has its day. How old women went on about their stomachs and young men their hearts... So, well, boy meets girl and banal beginnings soon mutate into a Mr and Mrs, man and wife, a Tara and a Basu, a wedding invite in your mail.

He remembered meeting Tara and Basu at some party, after the bombardment of intricately designed golden-lettered invitation cards, shehnai and sherwani and shlokas, and they looked, surprisingly, like they always did. No change. Sam looked on as if at a photograph, as if for proof of a them, as opposed to a him and a her.

The two sat together quietly in a corner, on a single sofa, and ate from one plate. Almost cheek to cheek, breathing in their oxygen from roughly the same spot, sighting and greeting the same people at the same time, smiles showing approximately the same number of teeth, displaying more or less the same quantity of happiness.

In courtships there is that phase when each jacks up their MRP. It wearied Sam now to think of that peacock phase when two people will pretend to talk to you while preening for each other, but between Basu and Tara no such event officially took place. Once when she tripped, Sam had been surprised at Basu's charged-up and silly-squeaky non-stop baby-talk of 'Theek aacho? Theek aacho?' It just seemed so wrong to have a large man worry so loudly and publicly about something so small and trivial as someone slipping on the floor and exaggerate it to a fracture or at least a sprain. And Tara looking all brave and deserving of a Param Vir Chakra, limping and saying, 'I am fine. Really, I am fine!'

Chemistry makes such asses of perfectly fine people because suddenly you don't know them anymore. Like their heads were squashed together and they have only one brain between them. Sam remembered how nosy he'd been about their house, about where they lived. So it was with great interest that he set out that evening, regretting only the lack of natural light. He had just met Delta then, and though he asked her to accompany him, had been relieved when she refused.

The road leading up to their house was strewn with slums. Naked children squatted by the sides, some saint could've made a real killing there. They had moved away from the city to the suburbs, Tara had told Sam, so that the children could be brought up 'properly'. It was a time domesticity and décor figured nowhere with Sam, but he noticed the khurja pottery, wrought-iron furniture, Banarasi cushion-covers and long wavy plants. It was a warm day and the AC non-functional but there were funny cigarettes, Patiala pegs and two small children who recited, badly, nursery rhymes in their mother-tongue.

Being out and so drunk after a long while, he went a little berserk. There were loud laughs, pork vindaloo, much puking in the basin, a long nap on some cool bed. When Sam woke up, he was the only guest left. He had exhausted the hospitality of Tara and Basu, who had jointly hosted Sam as much as any host in the world could host.

Sam had come away frowning, as if he was Sherlock Holmes at the beginning of a book, when the mystery was brought to him by a handsome woman in a horse carriage. He wanted someone to take him by his shoulders, sit him down and tell him in words he could understand who had he and she become together. The how and why of them. Tara and Basu were still with each other and gave every sign they meant to go on though they left each other alone too.

Lying in his hospital bed, Sam stared into the distance. There was something so super-gluey about husbands and wives. They fought and made up, laughed with each other and at each other. If one economised on yawns, the other offered her canines, molars and every single wisdom tooth for global scrutiny, as if even boredom should be a balancing act between them! There they'd be completing each other's sentences, vanishing in the same vehicle, calling the same kids 'our kids', talking about 'our bank balance' and 'our holiday' and 'our family home in Nainital'. Double dose of the same nasty medicine or two petals of a single rose. Couples were just so…static.

It didn't matter how people got together, it mattered that they stick it out. Delta had struck him like lightning, they had 'fallen in love', they had gone through the Tara-Basu stage of sounding like each other, of talking puzzlingly – for others who saw them as independent individuals – of the same things. History, home, hormones, that was a lot of H to share with anyone.

Which was why the platonic was so precious in a marriage. Why Delta held his hand and murmured 'Donx', dabbed his temple with lavender cologne. Why she used to yell murderously at him from time to time, talk about Sudan, Haiti and other places he had never heard of.

But sex was sex, wife or not. Cheating was as old as the hills, as old as marriage at any rate. Why, his was only a modern take on an old classic...

No, his brain shushed his tongue, no. Don't you know, he moved his lips ever so softly, there are things we don't talk about? And that little ear inside his head heard him all right.

22

Thank god for lower lips, thought Mira. In moments of deep crisis or even mild vexation, one could derive great solace from toying with it, chewing it, drawing blood. When Delta pushed her towards Sam so that he could get a full look at her belly, down came Mira's teeth on that bottom lip.

'He needs to see his baby,' Delta said firmly. 'That's his future.'

'Don't you see that upsets him?' countered Mira. 'You know he was ready to pay me to get rid of the baby. I didn't even know you were pregnant. But it is obvious he wants only your child. He asked me to kill mine, but your abortion almost killed him! Don't you *see?*'

'I have wronged him so much,' choked Delta. 'How will he ever forgive me?'

Ironic, thought Mira, that my hand strokes her comfortingly while she mourns the loss of her baby, a loss caused by my presence.

Delta and Mira operated cautiously along their new friendship. As if no spectre lay between them, no baby to be, only Sam. One of them sat with Sam while the other napped, bathed or went out with prescription slips. Between the two, it was Delta who spoke incessantly in soft sari-fold tones to Sam. The tender murmur sometimes woke Mira up at night, and she'd shift positions on the narrow bed and go back to sleep, reassured about the rightness of things.

Once or twice Mira was woken up by Delta, who'd say, 'You were lying on your belly, how could you?' And Mira would sleepily turn on her side while Delta covered her with a sheet. Mira would take this mothering personally, for her sake only, fairytale fetuses taking a backseat in her drowsiness.

The sorceress in the mirror had started to mist over, her horns glinting less and less. A tail swished idly behind as she puddled into whathaveIdone and the sweetest of sorryyyy. No longer her mother's rival, trying on lipsticks and wiles, but daddy's darling, penitent, childlike, with snot on the back of her hand. There was the little-girl oops about her now.

Mira studied Sam – the slope of his nose, the loosely curled fist by his side, even the arm she had drooled over – while he slept. She remembered the things he said, the things he did and immediately doubted her own ability to recap. *It's only my word against mine.* What if memories were inventions of a deserting mind? What if the things she thought he said and did were what *she* said and did? What if she willed him to say/do what he said/did? After all, it was only a word or two, a touch or two, and in a whole cosmos of words and touches spoken and touched and still being spoken and touched, what were a word or two, a touch or two?

Such opportunists they'd been, juxtaposing her 'goodness' against his 'badness'. If he had deceived, so had her ears. What business had skin retaining throbs well past the touch? Speech and touch were provocations of the moment, living in the moment for the moment. Tick-tock, gone. Skin, go back to peaches and cream.

She remembered too his abrupt silence, the lack of words that turned her homicidal. The hunger to have and to hold. No having, no holding. The no-rains, the no-calls, the can't-eats, the don't-dos, the no-no's, really, the nothings...Why *did* the mind fixate on nothings?

Serves her right, for thinking Sam's defection the end of the world. She was only thirty-something, for god's sake, there would be other cheats, other catastrophes, other occasions to rush in where Miras fear to tread. Staking her all on what? A tingle at the base of her spine? She conceded how her one moment of confidence in an entire lifetime of cowardice could be misconstrued as bold. Forward.

And, well, morality. Could she really accuse him of turning her into one of those? A loose woman. A fallen woman. As if women were teeth, to loosen and fall. Sam had been a bad choice. But *choice*. And had delivered exactly what she demanded of her future back then. To be wooed and wanted, wined and dined. To make 'the beast with two backs' as Shakespeare put it.

One man coming up. Man gone, case closed. She honestly couldn't mentally replay what they had done together, she and Sam. Had the hurt been as unbearable as she thought it then? Or had it just been her season for pain? God's way of saying, 'Thou shalt not escape thy share of pain'? Had they – Sam and she – by their coming together promised anything to each other? Had they harmed or benefited or usurped or appropriated?

Pop.

Two soap bubbles they'd been. Bursting at first touch.

'There is no us, no etymology of us. We can't be coded, catalogued, compiled or filed for future reference. We, except for

167

that brief moment in my head, did not exist.' Nothing and nobody was as wonderful as you wished them to be, she thought and felt her chest ease a little as some heart-space freed up. It occurred to her to get a cat. Or puppy. Or fish in a transparent bowl. For company when she got back home.

Mira picked up her phone and rang up the office. Though sitting here staring into space was fascinating, there was the little matter of her job. 'Hello, hello, Mira here. Mira Jacob. Can you put me on to admin?'

'Is that Mira madam? Madam, this is Mr Gowda here. I was going to call you, hee-hee, Mr Shetty asked me to.'

Christ, thought Mira, unable to converse further, *everyone knows my name... because I'm sacked!*

'Good you called me yourself, madam. Just a sec.'

'Hello,' said Mira into the sudden void.

'Hello,' said another voice.

'This is Mira...'

'I know it is you,' said the familiar voice, Mr Shetty's. 'Don't you want to come back?'

'I called up about that only, sir. I am thinking of taking some more leave. My mother is still unwell.'

'I am angry.'

'I am sorry, sir. My mother...'

'With you. For all this "sir" business. You know my name.'

'Actually, I don't, sir.'

Mr Shetty laughed a little. 'Can't you guess it?'

Mira felt the least she could do was try. 'Ravi? Shyam? Kapoor?'

'*Kapoor?*' asked Mr Shetty, his tone mercifully going back to the abrupt one he used with her at work. But then he added in his spongy new voice, 'It is Kailash.'

The matter of his name settled, Mira once again turned the subject to leave extensions. 'Sir...'

'Kailash.'

'I want a week more.'

'I want a week more, Kailash.'

'I want a week more, Kailash.'

'OK.'

'Shall I email you regarding this, sir, I mean, Kailash, or do I call personnel?'

'Nothing,' he continued in his novel, never-before-voiced voice, 'you do nothing. Not a thing. Look after your mother. And I shall wait.'

Mira rang off. Must be some new company policy, to call boss by first name.

In the evenings, after the doctor had been with his scary mutterings and notepad-waving, Delta insisted that Mira sit on the other side of Sam as she continued to croon to him. He frequently shut his eyes as if he couldn't bear to look at her anymore, then Delta turned to Mira and in the same soft voice narrated instances from their past. How they met, how they misunderstood, how they made up, how they fought for real, how they made up again, how they married despite the Lalan hostility, how they decided on interiors, vehicles, number of kids...

'And you know,' continued Delta as if talking to herself, 'we were no longer kids anymore but we still thought like the kids we were

when we met. We didn't want to grow up. Which is why Don
and I never planned a family for the longest time.'

So love's best when star-crossed, learnt Mira, who couldn
return the compliment of confessions. What could she say anyway
That she had envied just such attractions and attachments, tha
she had wanted to be one half of a couple, to partake of loving s
desperately that she had involuntarily poached on someone else
husband? And that here she was, having insinuated herself s
devilishly into their lives?

Mira sat there with the curious feeling of her pregnanc
turning into a real one. Under Delta's benevolent gaze, she bega
to bloom and at times felt like her body had begun to bear frui
She often caught herself rubbing her belly and even meeting Delta
indulgent eye.

She felt, one Sunday afternoon after Delta had warm-oiled he
hair and shampooed it and folded it onto her skull in radioactiv
waves from a magazine cover, like the surrogate mother who wa
ready to rent her womb to the man she could have loved and t
the woman he actually loved. That evening her stomach turne
transparent and she could see the baby. Such a spitting image c
its dad!

That was how she knew she really was pregnant. Even withou
the cushion, her stomach was distended. Breasts so tender to th
touch they perforated on soaping. In the mornings, she coul
barely insert toothbrush into mouth when her gorge rose. And i
rose at night too – she had therefore stopped brushing her teet
at night. Telling her that morning sickness was not really confine
to mornings, Delta got her lots of peppermint and that was a rea
relief. Sucking mint kept the nausea at bay.

'Gently,' Delta warned and Mira would lower herself slowly, slowly onto chair or bed. She had learnt to hold on to bars or support herself on the arm of the chair while sitting down or getting up and her legs had started to part of their own accord when she walked.

This could turn into madness, Mira warned herself after lowering oh so gently into the chair, because she could incubate *nothing*! She was bloated but whodunit? Water retention, gas, sour grapes? She should gather her wits while she may and quit ahead of a total nervous breakdown. The disease of wanting to please everybody in the world had crazed her, that was all.

How Mira laughed at herself, inaudibly of course, into the back of her hand, before going bananas and monitoring fetal movements hand on belly all over again. This was something no apparition had warned her about, the attack of the conscience, the mind's mouth that bit the very hand that fed it. However, Mira couldn't make light of peace. The serenity when she placed palm on stomach.

Sometimes Delta left them alone, her and Sam and their unborn baby, as if they were a family unit she would never be part of. Delta would look out the window or go out into the corridor or lock herself up in the loo, giving the other three time to commune with each other. At first, Mira's discomfort was too great to bear. But gradually, the lack of background bustle began to penetrate her consciousness and the Zen seconds followed.

Mira was then able to look at Sam's closed eyelids and remember desiring his baby so badly, she had to invent it. 'I was aching to carry your child, that's what brought me and you here to this point,' she'd whisper apologetically, imitating Delta's chatty casualness. 'How could anything that I wanted so badly end in such disgrace of nothing, of non-stop periods? That's what brought me here, not retaliation, but the desire to scare you into knowing what you missed, what you gave up when you walked out on me without a second look. You gave up this, this baby, this future, whatever we could have had. You not only gave up on me, you gave up on all we could have been to each other, the "we" we could have become. Someone gives up on your very essence, how can you move past that?

'Did you imagine I'd cry and fall at your feet to stop you from walking away? Wasn't that where all your creativity as a lover should have come into play – while persuading me how wrong you were for me?' she chided him. Closure would have made her less of a medical emergency!

'If these were earlier times or another part of the world, my family would've killed you for the dishonour you brought me,' she bickered with him behind Delta's back. 'If you had mentioned marriage, I could've sued you. Or cried rape and hunted you down with marigold garlands. I could have gone out there, made a hoo-ha, beaten my chest, sipped cyanide and dwindled away to nothing. I could have *died!*'

Sam said nothing, heard nothing. Mira sighed. If only he'd been *her* husband, she could have notified her family, his family, the police, registered him a missing person, lent her children to Maya and taken her dog for long walks. If he was her military-man husband, she could've declared him missing in action and claimed compensation from the central government. But what do you do when nobody walks away nowhere, leaving you with nothing?

Somehow, Delta knew the exact moment Mira's words tapered off. When Mira ran out of things to say to Sam, Delta would take over. And in the end that's what Sam understood – the unbroken continuity of attention directed at him. It pulled him out and along so that Leela-ben's visits saw him focus his eyes once again.

Much advice from Leela-ben was couched in little tales of Sam's babyhood and childhood – whooping cough, vaccines too late, chicken pox from a nursery school friend, fever that hit his brain causing convulsions that had Leela-ben running around town at midnight while Mr Shah had skipped town for a cricket match.

Leela-ben fussed over Mira too, bringing choice food for her. Pistachio nuts, Kashmiri apples, *panna* from really raw mangoes and sun-dried raisins. She had even begun to knit a shapeless something out of wool for the baby. It was as if while trying to convince Sam and the world, she had convinced herself too well to recover by now.

Not to be outdone in cottage industry, Delta took out her crochet needle. The sewing combat had an unspoken referee in Mira, who sat there dry-eyed and finger-crossed at such unbridled devotion to her imaginary offspring. Every night she prayed to make it real, that she carry the lie full-term. *Make my dream come true. Make their dream come true.* She expected God to appear before her in a burst of blinding brightness and grant her her wish. Oh, the divine racism of light that white.

'I'm only the channel, the vessel,' she would think virtuously. They – Sam and Delta – were the real parents of this baby. They wanted it, they believed in it, they very well *made* it! It was their child!

Then she would recoil from her own nonsense: indeed, and how would she explain the baby to the world, to society, to her parents, to the baby itself? A baby made entirely from thoughts would consign any mom to an asylum. She was carrying, yes, but she was carrying her own flesh, not flesh of her flesh.

She rued that she never tested her blood, never peed on chemical sticks, never checked whether they changed colour, whether she tested positive or negative. She had just presumed she wasn't pregnant because…But these things happen. Women bled their monthlies right up to labour. Could she shrug away motherhood only because it wasn't seemly? And if the baby existed, it justified everything – her 'feelings', her boo-boo, the randomness of it all, the urgent ululations of her womb. Parenting could be decided at either end. She could keep saying no, but the yes could meet her halfway down the other end.

She pointed at her belly, and addressed her invisible, judgmental audience: Hence. Therefore. Thus.

'My tummy hurts,' she fretted, riding the cramps, worrying Delta.

'It is the baby,' Delta went into a tailspin.

Mira's stomach clenched. Was it the baby?

'You must time the contractions. How many minutes apart? How intense? How…how?'

Mira was tempted to give up, give in. Her head giddy – or did the Earth just circle her? – she somehow stopped Delta from paging doctors. 'It is something I ate,' Mira told her and then lay an hour heroically disregarding her abdominal spasms until Delta's stomach stopped heaving for her.

'You know,' Delta confessed later, 'I think I'm suffering from sympathy pregnancy. Really. I've read the symptoms. I mean I am that tuned into you, or rather my stomach is that tuned into your stomach. Pregnancy can be infectious, I guess.'

Mira smiled weakly.

Sometimes when Delta told her kindly to spruce up before Sam woke up, Mira went back in time, to a childhood of sandalwood applied on face and neck carefully at night to 'bring forth the inner fairness' as if her real complexion lay trapped and required a Prince Charming made entirely of paste to break free. When she sneezed at school, sandalwood flew out of her nose. She put this paste on her dolls' faces, too, and shampooed their hair until their hair fell off so that she made little sparkly scarves for their bald heads before wheeling them out in a pram – discarded when Maya grew too large for it – for a little sunshine and vitamin D...

A neighbour had sneered at her bald dolls. 'They have cancer?'

That first month of Sam's silence had taken its toll on Mira in the form of extreme grooming. Ayurvedic massages on a slippery table with powder and oil, lying motionless to the Gayatri mantra. Of course, the first month she had the excuse that she was still waiting for Sam to come back and paw her. But the second month? That had been sheer indulgence on her part, as she told herself, to make her feel better. So her hair, her face, her neck, her shoulders, her legs, her hands, her feet got a makeover. Sam had granted her the Girlie Phase. She plucked her eyebrows, ripped off her sideburns. She even painted her nails.

What was it about men that made such asses of women, that they go about swapping sensible cotton undies for rash-giving lace scraps, sigh and pick at food, speak in a lisping new accent and hang little silver bells round and round their ankles? What was it about men that made such *women* of women?

In the first month after Sam left she had even done up her room. Indigo drapes and bedspreads, translucent vases reflecting the sky. Lots and lots of blue, Mira recalled and smiled, freaking Sam who happened to open an eye just then and catch her insane smile in his line of vision. For a moment he couldn't place her, then he did and the concerned eyelid came down with a clang.

~

23

'Happy birthday.'

'Thanks,' smiled Delta. Bringing in her birthday in a hospital ward with her husband's curvaceous mistress was a first for her. She longed to mother, to thicken for a cause, bounce her chest, deliver what her body was capable of delivering at this stage. Not to hear compliments on her figure, to be told she was 'well-maintained'. No one wants to age gracefully for a living.

Sam did not wish her at all and to make up for this Mira wished her many times over. She didn't have to actually look at Mira to notice her anxiety at this forced cohabitation and there were times she couldn't take her eyes off that belly with its secret inhabitant. Maybe she, Delta, should have brought all innovation to her own bed instead of offering it to sundry men. After all, with her craving every non-husband along the way, what she offered Sam had been cross-eyed lust at best.

'Need something?' Sam had asked once while stepping out for a stroll.

'Frozen peas,' she called out and watched his eyes glaze over with pleasure. And the day she had made a list of things to buy at the grocer's, he had gotten so aroused! When he returned from office and found her stirring something on the stove (even if it was only to reheat), he spooned her standing till she took him to bed. Like all men, mentally disabled by the sex-slave potential of a doormat. If she dropped her towel with deliberate eye contact, he walked out, but if she went 'oops', he went ape.

All her life Delta had mistaken love for lust and vice-versa so that she was often surprised in bed. If the two came in a package deal, she was yet to catch the bargain. There she'd be looking at the ceiling in a resigned manner, hoping he'd get it over with and then start to yell blue murder in astounded joy. Or she'd be with the man allotted to her, dry in the eye and elsewhere.

Actually up until she married, Delta had been the typically good girl of her mother's dreams. She had slept with no man before Sam and saw the folly of her inaction when she met an actor's eye in a film magazine and felt stirred beyond reason. At first she'd only wanted to cock-tease, to lust up someone to the point of madness, be flattered, take a bow. To be admired and adored, be an object of art, reveal a shoulder blade or collarbone, pelvic basin or pubic bone, lie or sit or stand or crouch, pose purely for purposes of homage.

Sam was simple, Sam was hers and loyal and faithful (until now), the father of all her future fetuses. Sex itself she'd managed to reduce to a matter of technical expertise, cha-cha-cha with a left kick. Foreplay she skipped, why draw it out? Quickies, she had presumed, were her thing. And she demanded only a change in location, not the man. Hence the dressing-table stool, the kitchen counter, the sturdy branch of a tree during a safari. Here, there, everywhere...

She'd been in her car, with rolled up dark-filmed windows, when she saw an old friend drive into a petrol bunk. Excited, she messaged him a 'hi', intending to get out and shout 'surprise'. She'd already arranged her fingers into a mock-gun to shoot him with when she saw him french-kiss his phone while reading her message.

Wow! She pulled out quietly, amazed she could make someone so happy so soon with so little, amazed at secret currents that energised, hinting at secret lives if she wanted. 'OK,' she took a deep breath. 'I'll do it, I'll do *affairs*.' Men everywhere would carry her marks and brandings, a weal from her nail, an indent of her teeth. She repeated lovers only if they managed to delight her with their detachment to her, if they respected the aspect of unfamiliarity so crucial to such unions, exchanged no pleasantries apart from those pertaining to their body parts in ménages of mutual consent. Every man wanted a whore and every woman had a whore in her. Eight men, eighty times. The sweet and sour of them exploding pure in the dead quiet of her tongue.

It was about the time Sam was to leave for Mysore that Delta finally decided she'd had enough of stolen splashes in hotel tubs. This insight had something, not everything, to do with the man she met through internet who joked, when she wanted to end their liaison, that they kill their respective spouses and get married for the heck of it. The kind of deadpan joke that can freak the shit out of anyone.

First came the fairy tale. He pinged her relentlessly till she agreed to meet. He said she was pretty, that her smile, her toes and eardrops were all pretty. The narcissist in her sat back, pleased. He made her feel small and silly, like a bauble. He shot down her wants, and she luxuriated in losing control. It excited her to enter a dark room she'd never been in before, blindfolded, to lie on unwashed sheets, wait for him and be used. To bend across a desk. Be handcuffed to a bed.

He was dismissive of prophylactics. They simply bored him. His boredom, an inherent part of his charm, translated now into attacks on her body. When she tried to tackle him sensibly on the matter, he admitted unabashedly that he wanted her pregnant, pregnant, pregnant. 'And then?' she asked, fascinated in a repulsed way.

'You keep it.' He shrugged. 'Or throw it.'

When she did not visibly react, he prattled on excitedly how they could pass off the child as her husband's (there had to be some advantage that she was a married woman, right?) or go together to a hospital to bump the baby off at the very last minute.

'A part of me growing inside you. You and me together in a way we cannot be.'

Still she said nothing, sat there silently, excited by his excitement but also mourning the demise of that romance. It had been hell to shake him off as kooks were often the best lays and she was one hundred per cent sure she'd find no one quite with his cruel elegance in bed. Sweet men, sensitive men, who cried when she came, who'd visit her with digestive biscuits at old-age homes, were not her type.

'I love you,' he said and she got over him in all those little parts inside of her that had not wanted to get over him. Such speeches were OK from a husband, marriages were where the word 'love' lived after all. But in any other man's mouth the word was a con. And to believe it the stuff of nightmares. Delta had a horror of turning irrevocably neurotic. It was OK to affect it, you were in control. She would *never* be that woman, heart in hand, smiling and crying at the same time. She had passed such women on the streets, watched them from her car window, feeling even as she stared that she was about to cross over and become them, a woman so in love she had to be sedated. Delta discovered something vital about herself that day, the day the madman said he 'loved' her: lust had been her way of warding off love, the kind that inhaled you in, crippled and killed.

As if to clinch the end he started to send her flowers, red roses the size of planets in bunches of two dozen. Delta hated it when sanity was forced upon her by default and she had to act like anybody else in a similar situation. He tried to woo her back, with inattention and then attention, but it was no longer her scene, to go mad on a mattress she knew not where. She terminated the trysts.

Guilt, buckets of it. Crawling down her like maggots. Guilt for loving more, loving less, loving wrong, loving too long. How to look into his eyes, her Sam's eyes, without splitting, splintering, scattering? The memory of her misdeeds drove her down, fast and furious, to a little town far south, the littlest town, actually, in the farthest south. So little that she occupied it sole and shriveled, bleeding head first, feet first, heart first to accommodate herself in such constant shrinkage. But it felt good to look herself in the eye.

She no longer surveyed the exposed parts of men speculatively. She noticed instead the dirty cuffs and collars of their shirts and their sweaty socks inside their shoes and calculated their laundry. She unhooked her 'Happy Hours' signboard and turned to Sam, good old Sam, the same whimsy that nudged her to multiple partners now leading her to monogamy. It comforted her to think that she could wander back into the marriage, pretending she had never left it. That she could at any time go back to being a desi housewife, complete with karvachauth kit.

She was back in her brain. How many ways were there to welcome a vagabond vagina home? She'd turned to Sam impulsively, 'Let's make a baby!'

But the joke was on her. Her husband had been equally busy it seemed. If only love was a quantity, Delta would have known if she was spending too much too soon or too little too late but as long as it remained a quality, she had no clue.

So there she was, entering her 31st year, suffering from birthday fatigue, huddling in a cake-refugee camp somewhere.

~

24

'Don't you mind?' Delta asked.

Unsure of what she was expected to mind or not mind, Mira went, 'Mmmm?'

'Putting on weight. But if you nurse the baby, I'm told, you can lose it all in a jiffy.'

Mira stuck to 'mmmm'. She'd been fat all her life, but it still felt good to hear there was a way she could lose it all in a jiffy.

'Will they let you fly?' asked Delta next. 'For fear of you going into labour.'

Mira said she was fairly certain they would let her fly.

'You know, you don't have to go at all. You can spend your maternity leave with us.' That was kindness coming at her from such unexpected quarters that Mira found all would-be responses thwarted. 'Of course,' Delta continued, 'I'm making it sound like a summer vacation. You will probably need your mother and all with you at the time.' She then asked awkwardly if she could touch her stomach, a request Mira couldn't refuse. 'Tell me when he kicks,' Delta said and Mira had to concoct occasions. She'd guard against the disappointment of Delta saying, 'But I don't feel it.'

Mira would have to say, 'Oh, may be he stopped now', and then Delta would say half-hopefully, 'I think I felt a slight twitch.' And sometimes, 'Maybe he doesn't like me.' To which Mira would respond by holding an invisible gun to her belly — jump, jump.

'You shouldn't feel bad,' Mira told Delta in her usual bumbling, longwinded way, 'There will be lots of other babies for the two of you. Maybe that baby wasn't meant to be ...'

Delta's response was fierce. 'I did not have an abortion, Mira. There was no baby to begin with.'

This took Mira deeper back into their life together — Sam and Delta's — which had never taken into account Mira's existence or Sam's betrayal of her. Mira had to comprehend Sam's fear of his talent going waste, Mr Lalan's income tweaking, Delta's mother's counter-wiles to Sam's mother's wiles... Mira began to doubt. Herself, her plan, even this loneliness she flamboyantly held against him. Hadn't it all been about her? Perhaps the exact degree of her earlier solitude determined the depth of her so-called love for him and exaggerated her sorrows, perhaps it was how happy he made her that super-sized the unhappiness that followed.

You are never what you really are to another person. It was impossible to see yourself the way another saw you, to affect the continuum only he could apply to you; not what you think you are in the sum total of all your past and present, but a kind of spillover of what he expects, wants, hopes for, thinks he deserves or needs at that point in time. So that his disappointments and delights concerning you are, in turn, so much a matter of his own dreams and expectations that they are, finally, nothing to do with you. It was nobody's fault she had love on her brain that day.

Poor Mira. Philosophy on the mind and pillow on stomach did not make for peace. Feeling superfluous, invoking memories that however real to her were only bogus to others, she felt more irrelevant than ever. But this time she could not take the redundancy personally, this time she saw the why and the what, all her FAQs finally answered. Sam's walkout was nothing to her walk-in. His arrogance nothing to her own, she who had tried to elbow her way in. May be all imposters felt like this, she thought – very real.

Mira knew what her gaffe was. Not the loving, not the lusting, not even the loathing which was a cunning way of continuing the loving, but the slow walk away. Timing was everything on the way in and out. Scorned women livened up literature, but in real life they were such a nuisance.

Let go, Mira.

Nightmares were making her a nervous wreck. The fear of being found out, the fear of causing more cardiac arrests, the fear of Delta's parents losing it and deciding to hire a hit-man in case hit-men were a status symbol in their social circles. What if the fetus took permanent residence if not in her body then in her brain? As it is, every dream of hers shaped a mouth. A small, perfect 'o' mouth of a baby. And from this 'o' came the cry. *Where are you?*

She thought, I have to tell the truth, whatever the damage, whatever the cost. Because there was no baby and that was the truth. But

I see you everywhere. Playground, school gates, in a stranger's lap, in a pram outside a shop. I look in on you in the middle of the night. Are you breathing, is the sheet kicked off, is the AC too cold? I'm here, hush, mommy is here.

Delta told her, 'I know a place where you can buy prams and nappies and feeding bottles with rubber nipples that can be easily sterilised.'

Maya called up, some nonsense about their mother having fallen somewhere. Apparently, Maya informed Mira coldly, amma was in great pain and demanding between IV-feeds Mira's presence by her bedside. Mira berated her mother silently on the timing. *I have enough on my plate. This is not your year by a long shot. This is just not your year. To go mad or die or have a hip fracture. I don't have the time, do you hear me?*

Her fear had splintered into a million living pieces, multiplying like lice but inside the head instead of out. Mira laid a vertical finger on her lips, pretended silence was as golden as libraries said it was. Now, back to the matter at hand.

I lean over and breathe in your talcum. Mmmm. I want to tickle your tummy but

The cotton sheet comes up empty in her hands.

Should she just make a general announcement and get it over with or take out an ad like those official name-change ones, saying, the abovementioned woman, Mira aka Myrrh Celestine Jacob, has never in her life carried another body within her body? Light, not easy to walk into.

But what if they arrest me under the Indian Penal Code – IPC something – for fraud or felony?

Still, truth was truth.

Is shamming a non-bailable offence?

A life sentence for a nine-month forgery very, very likely.

Moral of the story…

Stories aren't moral, the telling makes them so.

I run into the corridor, switch on the lights, shake out the sheets in the crib, throw down the pillow and teddy bear. The milk has curdled in the bottle into creamy cheese.

The vixens, cunning, manipulative and slimy, threw up their hands at Mira. The middle-women, compared to the middle-men, always got more flak! And why? Did vile really become viler via vagina? The vixens pursed their lips over stained teeth and laughed a laugh surprisingly so full of luscious vice that laugh-juice spurted all over their chins, but Mira held her hands to her ears and missed most of it.

Mommy is going to come clean.

~

25

Mira was rescued from her own nobility by Delta's friend, Stuti, who decided to take Delta out for the night as belated birthday partying though Delta protested vehemently. Mrs Shah had already been and Mrs Lalan came only to meet her daughter anyway.

'I'll take care of him,' Mira guaranteed grimly.

Stuti said to Delta in a peculiar voice, 'She says she will take care of him.'

Purple mascara shimmered like nits on Delta's eyelashes as she leaned over to plant a kiss on Sam's immobile lips. He did not kiss her back. Delta pretended not to mind. The truth was that for the life of her she couldn't remember when was the last time they kissed, really kissed. She remembered, of course, their first, as they had discussed it the day she told him she was pregnant. She refused to believe that had been a mistake – just two mouths in each other's way. But after that first thrilling encounter between their lips, kissing Sam was something she did in her sleep.

'Don't misbehave while I'm gone,' she called out gaily, and left with Stuti.

Mira waved back absently, having noticed the kiss – Delta's initiation of it and Sam's rejection of it. She regretted suddenly that she had not taught him to kiss her in Malayalam. To say oomma in a flying kiss that spoke.

She glanced at his mouth. Into which she had once crumbled deliciously. Well, thought Mira, if one measured a lifetime in kisses...kisses that happened, kisses that didn't, secret kisses, taboo kisses, dream kisses, day kisses. Raspberries from babies, the bold cousin who steals them, the same-sex classmate who wants to practice, air-kissing, passionately kissing the pillow. On cheeks, chin or the nape of your neck. Little plops of softness, consent or not.

There were many mwahs but not all achieved eternity. Mira rummaged through kisses past – which one was *her* kiss? Not Sam's. She could only remember the mechanics of his kiss, the way he shut his eyes and pursed his lips, tiptoed his tongue over hers and bit her teeth with his, but she couldn't taste it anymore. No, not that. Perhaps the one she gave her friend's dead mother lying on a mat on the floor of their house following a road accident? Most people had queued up to kiss the corpse and Mira had too. But when she did, a strange thing happened. Her mouth went condoling on its own, conveyed anger at the senseless nature of death itself and sought to infuse life. They were lips that lived a fuller life held against a dead cheek.

Kissing may be a cultural act but they brought faces together, people together, rubbed them like two stones for fire and had them populate. Mira looked at Sam and was tempted to kiss him again. To remind him of life, love, laughter, as a stupid CPR straight from the heart. But knew better than to act on an impulse that could only be misunderstood. *Little Miss Kissed, missing the kissing!* That's what he would think.

At about half past seven the power failed. Despite the distant hum of the generator, the main lights did not come on. Mira guessed power must be pawned to surgery theatres where life-saving procedures were underway. A nurse distributed candles. Placing the candle on the bedside table and a little unnerved by the deepening silence and darkness, Mira joked, 'Alone at last.'

Not surprisingly, Sam stayed mum. Of late he had begun to talk and Mrs Shah was the main recipient of these low murmurs. He had also started to roll his eyes at Delta's sappy tales of their togetherness. And the one time that Mira gave him the bedpan, there had been no eye contact. Who could blame him, she thought. It wasn't as if he hunted down her heart and shot it point-blank, she had hung her heart on the nozzle of his gun.

She coughed. He did not grab the chance to feel up her forehead for 'flu. And they had been such a happy couple for that heartbeat! 'How are you feeling?' she asked, little expecting him to engage in civil dialogue.

Maybe the silences had piled up too much inside of him, maybe it was Delta's absence, maybe in his own way he was thankful to Mira, maybe it was no longer possible to be dignified with someone who timed his motions, but he thought it time to break his self-imposed silence. 'How am I supposed to bloody feel?'

'You don't want me here,' she declared with long gaps between the words and he wanted to punch her in the nose for this exaggerated care. He who had taken her with his swagger, his smooth lines, now lay cadaverous and still, stamped 'handle with care' on the head. The man in him moaned in shame.

Mira took a deep breath and heard herself say, 'You didn't want me from that first time itself. I get it, I mean I got it. You won't talk to me! I am not good enough even for an explanation!' She remembered going into shock, for offering herself to the wrong man. 'When you left...it was like a death in the family,' she stated. She sensed tears, she sensed a fit coming on, but her trembling voice had more to say. 'You dared to turn your back on this, on us, on what I would never do with another man. I had never, *never*, felt that way before. All I asked was for a connect, but knowing it was all on my side was too...' She felt then a small frisson of awareness. Without looking at him she knew he was looking at her properly, that she had at last caught his attention.

'I no longer believe you will do your best by me, you are so upfront about not being there for me, like it's a virtue or something...' She looked at him then and instantly felt their ages change. When they met was perhaps the only time they'd been the same age, after which he had grown younger and younger. Strange, how changing ages keep the sum total of years between two people roughly the same. Here she was, ninety in her head.

'You don't need me,' she mumbled, feeling like an idiot. 'You have all the friends you need. I mean...' Thankfully, he did not enquire as to what she meant for she knew not what she was going to say or think.

The candle wick began to dance, taking the shadows in the room now here, now there. They watched the drop of wax poised over the flame buck back into itself at the last moment. In the flickering light, Sam's eyes curved like berries.

She said softly, forgivingly, 'If you can't stretch your heart, you can't.'

'Heart-fart,' he snorted. 'Why don't you admit you were waiting for some sucker to come and get suckered? Maybe you couldn't get the man you wanted so you thought you'd take it out on someone, on me. After all, I was nice and anonymous. I just had to put out my hand and you jumped right in. You asked me nothing, not once if I was married. You just needed a man for the night! You were horny, but no that would be too much to own up, that you are a normal woman with normal desires. Maybe you needed a man because you were broody, I don't know. Or,' he tried to sit up in his excitement, 'because of your saint complex, you couldn't do it without "falling in love"'.

No, no, no, no, no. *Nooo.* Mira couldn't honestly remember anymore why she had hated him so much at one time. Or loved him so much before that. Love at first sight, hate at last sight – in the middle sputter-sputter, put on generator the Great Fizzle Out.

Sam let the rage subside and listened to his heart, its steady, reassuring beat. She had responded, been *available*, did she not expect to be bamboozled a bit? He said through gritted teeth, 'We had sex, okay? Sex. Men and women get together and have sex all the time. That's what they do.'

'Don't tell me that,' she said, fixing her elbows on his bed, her eyes dead serious. 'Sex is not as kneejerk as everyone makes it out to be. I have thought about it a lot, you know.' God, she had done little else. 'There is the smiling and the looking and the thinking and the planning and...'

'The phone calls, the flowers, the dinners, the borrowed bed,' he finished for her, manfully straddling the other side of the seesaw. Suddenly he peered at her, unsure. 'It was...mutual, right? You *wanted* to sleep with me?' He lay back before she could answer, adding, 'Of course. Of course it was.'

They both sat silently, thinking about sex in general and sex in particular. When sex had meant they were alive on such and such day with such and such person somewhere on a spot of earth when it didn't matter where. Terra totally infirma.

'Okay, we had an affair. Half an affair at any rate.'

'No, no,' Mira gave in gracefully. 'We had sex.'

That's the thing with men, she learnt. When you talk of love, they reduce it to a bodily function. They fish for compliments, for flattery, for only-yous and nobody-else, and the yes-yes-yes in growing pitch. You sit there with 'peel-me' stamped on your forehead like a flamboyant onion, hoping he can see through skin and read everything scribbled on the back of your soul when he can just about locate your bra hook...

Sam shrugged. 'I can use a condom, you can be on the Pill, we can both abstain and the sperm still finds the ovum.'

This made Mira cringe; she had never actually heard the word 'sperm' spoken aloud. Best to change the subject. She fixed him with a devoted look and laughed a self-deprecating laugh. 'You can touch a woman so casually! Your world doesn't fall apart. I want to be like that.'

'You don't want to be like that,' he said heavily, thinking how you could not touch someone else and then go back to touching your wife like you used to. 'And I am not like that either. Not really.'

'But you wanted so little of me,' she was still admiring. 'I mean, I haven't even thought what I could give anyone, any man, in terms of my body. I have so much more...' her voice trailed away. She thought how necessary it had been to see him laugh, to say things to him to outrage his eyes, to confide in him, to have him confide in her the littlest, goriest detail about himself that she was ready to listen without ever being shocked, and to make him happy, happier than he'd ever been. She would have held his hand in every way, been his, in his corner, slain his dragons, kissed his bruises better, sung him to sleep…

'I can't believe this happened,' she waved a hand around, saying sincerely, 'I can't believe *you*. Nothing comes between you and *you*.'

Sam felt goaded into some kind of apology yet again. 'I should not have…loved you.'

She did not reply for she did not know if she truly regretted him. When a seam picked and you unraveled at such speed, the re-raveling carried you into a different shape. Love *had* liberated her for a while there, trapezed her soul into the wild unknown without a safety net. She had always been so controlled, so knowing of herself, and then she had washed out on a sea of feelings, been someone else, someone she had never known, would never have been without Sam. *A defrosting of me.* Her heart did travel over to another, things had gotten…inter-heart. She had arched back her neck for love bites and met a man's unshaven chin at the end of the day. She had felt Eve haunt her finger as she crooked it. Every woman needed to detonate thus, Mira thought virtuously, at least once in a lifetime. In a thisismyman, comewhatmay, I'llkillmyself way, avoiding terraces because their edges begged her to jump off. It was called primary education of the heart.

'Hello, I am Mira,' she said, putting out a hand.

'Sam. Nice to meet you.' He shook hands with her. 'Is your name really…?'

'Myrrh? Yes.'

'I never knew.'

She chided pleasantly, 'You came in saying bye, where was the time to tell you anything?'

They smiled at each other again, this time more fully, happy after a long time, and then found they couldn't stop smiling as they went on smiling at each other, at the TV, at the window, floor, ceiling till it looked like the smiles would have to be surgically removed from their faces.

Pax. The room was fitted instantly with little white flags all over. When an orderly wheeled in Sam's dinner, Mira scooped blanched this and boiled that on to a plate for him.

'I can eat on my own,' he protested, but she settled down by his pillow and prepared to feed him like Delta always did. It had been so exhilarating, that journey from the unfamiliar to intimacy. Now she had to find a way to make the reverse drive equally goose-bumpy, until they were two strangers again with polite smiles and half-mast eyes.

With each spoonful, she made little maternal sounds, but it was as she fed him his soup – blowing unbecomingly into the spoon – that her inherent clumsiness reared its head. The bowl upturned and most of the burning hot liquid splattered on to her stomach. 'I am sorry. Have I hurt you, the baby...?' he gasped.

'No,' she said, as the cushion sponged up the soup nicely.

Sam said out of the blue, 'You know, you don't show at all.'

Mira shot him a startled-doe look. What did he mean? Did he guess? Did he know? Had the near-death experience kick-started his IQ?

'Some women,' he continued condescendingly, 'don't.'

Mira sat up straight, sticking out her tummy, her cushion. Nothing doing. Sam still smiled fondly at her stomach as if it was freshly liposuctioned. She retired to the loo, took out the smelly cushion (she could not very well wash it and drip-dry it before its real parents, could she?), mopped up the soup the best she could and discovered that, horror of horrors, her period had arrived all pre-punctual and wide-eyed. But stress brought that. Bloodshed in her undies. She patted a pad into place and thought how she was right and wrong about everything.

'Sam,' she said, looking like Emperor Ashoka among the corpses that last day; she should never have declared war on Sam. His face lost its genial look. She hurried on, 'I will do anything, *anything*, to make your life go back to what it was.'

'What can you do now?'

'Anything,' she repeated, tears splashing down her cheeks left and right.

'Could you ...? No, you can't.'

'I can,' she said urgently. Because whatever it was, she *could*. He shook his head, so she took him by his shoulders and shook him hard, uncaring of the menacing tubes attached to him. 'I can,' she screamed into his face.

~

26

Stuti glanced at Delta. It was obvious her husband was playing around. The woman sitting by Sam's bed, bump and all, was having his baby, and unlike Delta's, this was an authentic baby.

The night she walked out on Sam, Delta had landed up distraught at Stuti's house. 'But why walk out of your own home?' Stuti asked, having fought bitterly to gain this one-room tenement from her parsimonious ex-husband. Turned out, Delta thought grand gestures her domain now that she was officially a betrayed being.

First thing next morning she called up Sam, lying through her teeth about an abortion – well, she did abort it from her imagination. Over a gastronomically confusing breakfast of vada-naan with blueberry sauce, Delta declared she would never speak about Sam again. 'Can't even make his mother come, motherfucker!' she sneered. But when Stuti spoke of other things, Delta's eyes wandered out of the room. They were both at the gym when she got the call about Sam's heart attack

Now that Stuti had caught a glimpse of the rival, she geared up for a display of touching loyalty to Delta. But before Stuti could begin to bitch about Mira, Delta asked her disinterestedly, 'Where are we going?' When Stuti named a new bar in the city,

Delta nodded. She loved to check out the interiors of any new place in town.

Delta wrinkled her nose at the chi-chi door. Elaborate exteriors only voiced deep-seated insecurity. 'I love to dance,' Stuti said, and proceeded to dance wildly, her hips coming up hard like metal against magnet and her lips pushed back like a receding hairline so that the bald gums shone pink in the light. Delta sipped her drink, nibbled at the salted peanuts and watched her friend dance.

The drums were sinister, with a kind of thunder and lightning in it that only mean music has. The drummers sounded pissed as hell and were infecting everyone with their fury. Stuti continued to dance. Three or four men walked in then and seemed a bit surprised to see a fat disjointed woman looking so...happy. Hers was not a figure for abbreviated T-shirts but Stuti wore them even to sleep. Preferably in pink or purple two sizes too small like insomnia shrank her lycra.

A man began to jiggle in front of her friend. For a moment Delta felt relief – it looked kind of alright to have a partner in this dim-lit bar. It was dancing *alone* and with that amount of happiness on your face that seemed not OK. But her friend was twitching away from him in a moment and dancing again – every one of her movements frankly uncoordinated – *with no one at all*. Can't she at least pretend to dance with this man if she must dance in the first place? Is there any harm in faking a bit of coordination and grace? No, she was just undulating towards the aisle next and turning towards Delta with a mad glint in her eye.

'Oh no, I won't! No way will I leave this cozy little plastic chair,' she protested, but Stuti had boogied her way to Delta's knee and now stood shivering ecstatically at her. She was mad! And she did not care! Cool down, she wanted to tell Stuti. But Stuti tugged hard and Delta was off her seat in a minute and standing there foolishly grinning at no one in particular.

Now that she was standing, Delta saw no harm in continuing to stand. So she stood and then loosened her shoulders this way and that as if in time to the music. Then Stuti narrowed her eyes into hers and Delta felt like she was reentering a familiar tunnel. A strange kind of shake started deep inside her, a rumble and a clawing. Her feet, especially the soles, began to itch like a pair of monkeys. She was alone again, alone in an exciting way, no one expected her and she expected no one. And just like that she felt…dancy!

Two hours of shimmy-shake parched her throat. Delta made for the bar, weaving her way through a happy mass of people. A man stepped out of the smoke. 'Hi,' he smiled. An admiring glance top to toe. 'Are you an athlete?'

She wrinkled her nose. 'A couch potato.'

He shrugged a 'whatever', saying, 'You are hot.'

And you are a thermometer, she hazarded a guess. 'What,' she enquired conversationally, 'is your best sex with the wife?'

'In the shower,' he said promptly. 'Half-standing, half-sitting.'

'The best you'll get out of me is a hand-job, fully clothed,' she told him matter-of-factly. *Yeah, I know, better wifey in the shower.*

Delta was back on the dance floor in no time. Piss off, playboy. It was all in the chase. *She* decided when. *She* decided how. *She* decided where and who. It had to be a man-woman moment, the yen, yes, but, first of all, the scenting and only then the change in breathing. She boxed an imaginary foe with her fist. 'And,' she thought with such relish that she almost fainted, 'I'm back.'

Gradually the music ceased and the two friends grew tired – as Stuti said, 'I still love rock n' roll but just don't put another dime in the damn jukebox' – and collapsed on the landing outside, giggly as the night air straight tickled their armpits. Glad and mad, with the drums still pounding the back of their skins, they sat there reciting nursery rhymes, feeling neither man nor woman but really small children.

'Listen,' she told Stuti, 'that was…' Then she shook her head because she plain forgot what she wanted to say. Instead she said in a clear voice into the night, 'Lapis lazuli', and Stuti turned to her with shiny eyes. Back in college they both thought this the most poetic of words in the world.

Delta became vaguely aware that something had gone wrong in the minute weft and weave of her brain in the past few minutes. That some dearly held thought or principle had come undone. She frowned and then felt her brow clear. The breeze, brandy and a bandicoot man – sometimes a woman can take only this much before her brain clams up.

The next morning Delta came in late, yawning hugely at Sam and Mira. 'I had the time of my life!' she spoke with her mouth still wide open. 'Did you have breakfast?'

Sam and Mira shook their heads, not looking at each other. For the first time the pair felt guilty about colluding, about doing something behind her back.

Delta caught hold of Mira's hand. 'Let's go get a bite. We will get him a doughnut.' She winked at Sam. 'Heart attack over!'

Usually Mira would have protested at leaving the patient alone, at the upgrade in status to equal etc but now she silently picked up her handbag. Smoothing the disproportionate rear that doomed her to eternal imbalance through her journey on earth, Mira meekly followed Delta out to a café across the road.

~

27

The sun is everywhere. Ants queue up for fallen sugar cubes. The strong smell of coffee aims straight for that last little zzzzz in the brain. The women note the lime and green chillies spiked to the café door to ward off evil because there is something inherently dangerous in wanting too much.

Yet they want. To be wanted, to be chased, to be serenaded, to be sighed over, to worship, to enslave, to pine. In sunlight or moonlight. In bed or out.

Mira is the one with pangs as she faces her ex-lover's wife. Will she be able to convince, hadn't she already shot her credibility to pieces, did anyone listen to women of easy virtue anyway and *ooofff* what coffee to choose…She looks up at her audience to find it, oddly enough, shaky. And saying something in a voice that broke like an adolescent boy's. 'Thank you so much!'

'Welcome so much!' says Mira automatically.

They look at each other emotionally. 'You know what I mean, right?'

No, owns Mira readily, she doesn't.

Delta wields her straw impatiently; she still can't get over last night. Stuti's hips coming unhinged that way, the unstoppable dancing, the post-midnight nirvana. 'You know, I had decided I would love only him from now on. That he was worth…'

Fidelity. The word hovers dead polite over the sugar sachets and the sour-cream something looping around the ceramic plate between them.

'And you know how *strict* he is in the bedroom. So no-nononsense.'

'I don't know,' Mira demurs in soft, dulcet tones that one used for wedding vows. One time she had slept with this woman's husband. Once upon a time, long, long ago. Did that make her an expert on Sam or sex? She had thought herself touched by Midas, that she was finally the gold at somebody's fingertips, but how to say this to…Mrs Midas?

'Because he slept with you we are equals now.' Delta smiles, thinks of her breasts being cupped…She frowns. Why cupped, why not saucered?

Mira says, 'I have something to say that will take you running back to Sam.'

'Nothing will. Not even these funky sneakers of mine.' Delta gives a sly smile. 'Sam is OK. He was just very, very respectable.'

Mira is puzzled. 'Isn't that a good thing?'

'Too good. He was congenitally faithful, that was the only thing wrong with him! You cured him of that.'

'I have something to tell you.'

'Don't tell me,' howls Delta. 'Last night, you and Sam…'

The prude in Mira tightens the drawstrings of her mouth in one sharp jerk. 'Never with a married man!'

Delta asks super-sweetly, 'Never?'

Mira says with dignity, 'He forgot to tell me he was married.'

'Men can be such bastards,' Delta says amiably, her eyes circling the café to assess clothes, hairstyles, man-boobs, moobs, whatever ... 'So you are saying that you don't love him anymore?'

Mira shakes her head. Love him? All her love had gone into not hating him.

Ah, the double standards of singles, marvels Delta, remarking lightly, 'How nice to know where and when and how much to love.'

Suddenly Mira feels everything die on her – all the lovely colours slapped on that morning, her earrings, the three-tiered kurta with the baby frill at its hem, the henna tattoo on her thigh where no one can see. She buries her face in her hands. 'I loved him!' whispers Mira fiercely. 'I loved him! I loved him!' Alas, her love is no longer predestined or eternal, but vulgar, dirty, doomed, forbidden, indecent and adulterous.

'It was just that one night ...' says Mira but maybe it came out all wrong, like she wanted a lifetime of Sam and got only a spoonful.

'You got lucky,' snorts Delta.

Mira sees the irony of being comforted by this woman of all women so she collects herself, thought by thought, enough to declare, 'The thing is ...'

'To shop for maternity wear.' Because that is the truth, Delta thinks, the baby en route.

'The thing is this, I am not pregnant.'

As Delta stares, Mira repeats Sam's words. What he asked her to say to his wife.

'I. Am. Not. Pregnant.'

This is what he had told her the previous night, in tight, damage-control mode:

'Go have the baby somewhere, anywhere, but tell everyone that you were mad, so mad that you came here lying that you are carrying my baby. For revenge. Let everyone think you were that desperate for me. If Delta thinks you lied and that there is no baby, our marriage will be back on track. I mean, I've embarrassed you and you've embarrassed me. Let's just go back to embarrassing ourselves on our own now!'

'What do I say about this?' she had pointed at her bump, before remembering what it was.

'You are a big fat woman, Mira. Just say it is your paunch. In fact, you looked like this only when we met. Say this is not a baby, I just ate too much. Say anything. Who cares! As if anyone is a detective here.'

Mira stared at her former beloved, such a hoarder of himself, and forgot forever every kiss, every grope, every hope. He was not the man in her past, there was no man in her past, her nipples had never been his rosary beads. She could therefore demand bitterly that in return he never get in touch with her (or the baby!) ever again, that she would lie for him and then walk into the sunset *alone*.

He had only been too happy to obey. 'Deal.' He had grazed her palm with his solemnly, moistly, touching her voluntarily after seven long months of total skin drought. 'Tell this one lie and disappear. If you love me like you say you do, just give me back my life. Go.'

And Mira had looked at him, couldn't, in fact, take her eyes off him as he asked for his life back, this man she had wanted to give her life to. How she had sulked at the lack of him! He crossed his arms on his chest, his hands curling in fists. Arms still to die for, ending in such self-protective palms, taking good care of himself. He was in good hands, his own.

'Bye,' he said.

A new endearment, said with the same urgency and passion as all the previous sweet nothings. There, she could see herself dead and buried in the left side of his brain. On her tombstone he had inscribed: *mea culpa*. And she lay there without birdsong or sunlight, the onetime mistake of a married man.

Left holding the baby. Left to walk away finally, chat up the wife, say what she was asked to say. 'I am not pregnant.' Quote, unquote.

Mira hears a cackle. Maybe a devil-woman somewhere, who was never satisfied culling goodness or souls like her dimwit devil husband who went around demanding such things childlike, on an impulse, with a boyish grin: *take all that's on me, but hand in your soul, hand in your soul.* But his wife knows better: rich creamy sanity over a crummy old soul any day. A devil-woman who gorged solely on sanities, picking delicately between the multiple layers of lunacy, waiting patiently for women – standing, sitting, kneeling, knitting women – to snap. Who broke plates inside your head all day long and screeched at you to pick up the pieces. '*Pick up the pieces.*' Who fed off female meltdowns, their mourning and the mildew between their legs.

'*Ready or not?*' she calls out now.

'Not,' Mira pulls poltergeist leg. A baby cries in the distance. Hers? Somebody's? She imagines a botched MTP. Nice and red. Trickling down two pale thighs.

Showgirls kick up their toes in a straight chorus line, her heroines of the hereafter in their sepia portraits in smoky nightclubs, their upper lip surging blood red and thirsty while the lower sticks out guiltily for sleeping with the wrong man again, damn. The temptresses get their sycophants, yes, but what do they know about the suffering of the living suck-ups, of the dementia that shines brighter than their diamante?

No baby? Are you sure?

And milk jabs her nipples like needles.

'Are you lying to me now?' Delta is asking, still not able to pull the trigger on the whole baby bit. 'Will you just go ahead and have the baby somewhere? Do I have to fear your return, you know, the sequel?'

Mira looks back at Delta steadily, sucks in her belly and sits up straight. 'I lied.' Small, baby lies. Each lie a pacifier in the mouth. 'Come,' she says, taking Delta into the loo. There she removes the still sodden, soupy, stinky cushion and drops it into the trashcan. 'See.'

'We both tricked Sam!' cries Delta, clapping her hands like a child.

Mira feels, for the first time, that Sam is none of her business. That now on, praise the lord, Sam and Delta are on their own, their life – together/separate – *their* concern. Mira could see a lot of life ahead of her, of going back to work, giving it back to those superior mini-skirted women, of visiting mother back home, of taking note of a man some day, of going by what he puts on record, of superimposing Sam, of hinting to her yellow-faced landlady which E of her husband's was MC square, of actually enjoying the calm and quiet that comes from being by self.

She also has to thank Sam for the lesson he'd been, for being a microcosm sample of how the world could screw her if she let it. The good men and the bad men are always going to be shuffled up together, she has to separate the two, pick the better man. Oh, she looks forward to so many things: the first raindrop, the first rainbow, the first reindeer cardboard cutout of the Christmas season in a shop window. She hasn't laughed for so long, she can't wait to hear the first joke, but first…Exit Left.

'You do know,' brags Delta in a subdued way after they reclaim their chairs, 'I have been unfaithful to Sam.'

'Once?' hopes Mira.

'Many, many times.'

To Mira, Delta seems markedly sad at that moment, like she wants to be stopped or scolded or something. Why can't they take time off to fix this thing between them, instead of digressing? Because this is easier, Mira gets it. Some marriages are just a taxidermist's delight. And the thing is, Delta's discovery of Sam's trespass and Sam's future discovery of hers are labeled all wrong. Mira wants to bang their heads together; the cheating is in the lying, not the fucking. Getting caught, now *that* would be infidelity! Better lie next time. Mira smiles. A one-time hook-up is more honest than a lifetime of marriage.

Mira, miscast as Vishwamitra's Menaka, contemplates the pastry before them. She has never seen Delta eat. During their enforced stay in the hospital while caring for Sam, there had been no cozy meals between them. If there was one thing Mira couldn't abide, it was hunger. She thought a lot about famines, women fasting for spouses and fad diets, usually while cleaning up the fridge with her mouth…

Mira starts to eat what's before them, she is after all eating for two, when her mobile beeps. The message: 'Chat with anyone anywhere in the world for one rupee only!' But Mira looks up coyly and lies — only to clarify that she is no longer crushing on Sam, that she had reclaimed all parts of her, especially the hormonal — to Delta, 'Should be going home. A friend is coming to Bangalore soon and says he can't wait to see me.'

'Must be drunk, watching porn,' scoffs Delta good-naturedly. 'Oh go on, infatuate.'

Mira watches Delta fish out a cigarette and a single thought vacuum-cleans the sunshine from the trees and the traffic and brings it dancing to their table: *she believes me, I have won, Sam and I have won.* For if she thought Mira with child she wouldn't light up, as simple as that.

Akshara-pishachu, word-monster, that's what her father used to call her fondly when she gobbled up paras and paras of History and Hindi, by-hearting without understanding. Maya called her 'mugger' because she could 'mug' just about anything. And now she had brought this talent to anti-truths. But as Mira found out, in her finite wisdom, lies loved to merry-go-round, that once you start, you can't stop.

Delta has long left. Back to the patient, her husband, Sam, Donx. And that's all for the best. For marriages to succeed, men and women should put each other first. Miras come and go, providing entertainment, such social workers, the real champions of marriages, spreading their legs quietly, discreetly, on demand, but marriages are the original *cul de sacs.*

She is fine. From the start he was never a must. Nothing is a must except your own life for you to go on living. The sun is still everywhere. Blithe spirits continue to do what they do best, be blithe. Mira sits there alone, holding her head in her hands to stop its shaking, saying again and again that she is not expecting, never was. Only, she doesn't know whether she is lying like she promised to or telling the truth like she wants to.

There, can you hear it, the patter of tiny feet?

There is no baby, there never was and there never will be, OK? There wouldn't be, there couldn't be…

Couldn't? Are you sure? A hundred percent? Lock kar diya jaaye?

Her phone beeps again. Must be the talk-time guys, she thinks, but no, it is…Littleshit! 'When r u coming back? Beginning 2 miss u.'

Omygod, thinks Mira, it is Sam! No, not Sam, this is not his number anymore. It's the wrong number calling back. 'Do I know you?' she texts, wondering how she could explain to a total stranger her melodramatic outpourings, sometimes at midnight. Two minutes on comes the reply: 'All that fresh air has made you forget me ☹…yours, Kailash'

Kailash? Kailash??? Sam said he had returned his phone to the Bangalore office, and the phone is now…Mr Shetty's! What must Mr Shetty, er, Kailash, think of her? Mira tries in vain to remember the exact wordings of every message she ever sent this Sam/Littleshit/Kailash. Her mind is blessedly blank.

They clear the coffee things and a hand-holding couple eyes her discreetly, wondering when she'd vacate the table for them so they can carry on with their cooing more comfortably.

How can I go, Mira worries, leaving my baby behind?

'It doesn't exist,' comes the demoness's bored voice.

Why not? I am a Succubus just like you, aren't I? I can make them on demand.

The demoness laughs so loud and so long that Mira's hair flies backward in that venomous breeze. She brings her face close to Mira's, her breath foul. 'Not even a sub-Succubus. You did not seduce, you were seduced, you loser. The sperm came to you by fluke, but you could not keep it alive between your legs. It was dead when the Incubi came. Dead! He could impregnate no human woman with it. We needed you, we treated you as our own and what did we get? *No baby!* Mind you I have unleashed a million Succubi since then and, boy, do they know how to party!'

Mira says sorry and begging-your-pardon and thank you though she knows she will always doubt the demoness's word on the subject of her baby. Could she not feel it crawl on its fours inside her? But best to go with the flow. 'Bye then,' she says uncertainly, changing the subject.

'You can't say bye to yourself.'

I can't say bye to myself.

She makes a run for it then. Reaches the road, hails a cab, slumps in the backseat without looking back once. One thing at a time, she tells herself, catching her breath: she has a flight to catch. You can be a basket case anytime you want, but planes, they have deadlines.

All quiet now, inside her head the sweet rustle of hush. Dealing with desire – for a man, revenge, anything – can be so draining! That reminds her, she will have to reply to Mr Shetty, can't keep him hanging forever. Why not? But. What can she say? And what if she mis-spells while texting? He may get over this fit, he won't forget a typo. 'Maybe I can dangle him about a bit,' she thinks vaguely, 'try to use him.' For which she will have to rush into the car park like Prerna used to do and see what his eyes look like under those spectacles. Owing to the state of her soul she wouldn't be able to cook and owing to the state of his stomach he wouldn't be able to eat. Still. He is – what do they call it? – an option. Like that doctor chap, Amit. Like every other man in the world. Like every man in the world is to every woman in the world.

Mumbai continues to rush past in people, lampposts, glitzy salons, handcarts of food and a slither of sea now and then. Had she really arrived here a lifetime ago frothing at the heart? She feels older now. Not old, mind you, just older. A brief stopover in la-la-land and now she must return. All rebels in No-Nonsense Land were granted amnesty, she'd heard it that morning on the radio.

Perhaps all practical women begin as impractical little girls.

~

Not without

Madhavi Mahadevan and Keerti Ramachandra.
Shaji.
And Sam's terrace.

~